HIS PREGNANT ROYAL BRIDE

BY
AMY RUTTAN

MILLS & BOON®

First published in Great Britain
By Mills & Boon, an imprint of HarperCollins Publishers
1 London Bridge Street, London, SE1 9GF

Large Print edition 2017

© 2017 Amy Ruttan

ISBN: 978-0-263-06721-7

Our policy is to use papers that are natural, renewable
and recyclable products and made from wood grown
in sustainable forests. The logging and manufacturing
processes conform to the legal environmental
regulations of the country of origin.

Printed and bound in Great Britain
by CPI Antony Rowe, Chippenham, Wiltshire

Royal Spring Babies

*Unexpected royal heirs
for two Italian princes!*

Dante and Enzo Affini,
Venice's hottest doctors, have a secret…
they're also Italian princes! Now, to save
their inheritance and the family name,
they'll need to marry and produce heirs—*stat*!

For Nurses Shay Labadie
and Aubrey Henderson a six-month stint
in Italy teaching new nurses is the escape
they both need. But as romance blooms in
the spring sunshine they find themselves
with new roles entirely…as royal mums!

Read Dante's story in
His Pregnant Royal Bride
by Amy Ruttan

Read Enzo's story in
Baby Surprise for the Doctor Prince
by Robin Gianna

Available now!

Dear Reader,

Thank you for picking up a copy of *His Pregnant Royal Bride*.

I was privileged to write this duet with one of my absolute favourite people, Robin Gianna. When our editor asked if I wanted to write a duet with her as my fourteenth book for Mills & Boon Medical Romance I answered with a resounding *yes!*

The best part of writing this duet was when Robin, me and our editor were all at the RWA Nationals conference in San Diego and we got to hash out the timeline and plot soaking in the sun by the pool. Those kinds of editorial meetings don't happen very often!

Nurse practitioner Shay Labadie has had a pretty rough hand in life, but it doesn't deter her from doing work all over the world, bringing medicine to those in need. She's quite admirable, and her first name is after a friend whom I also find admirable.

Dr Dante Affini has also been dealt several blows, but has led more of a charmed life being an Italian prince. Though *he* thinks it's far from charming— and after a one-night stand leaves Shay with a baby *she* thinks he's not her Prince Charming either.

I hope you enjoy Shay and Dante's story.

I love hearing from readers, so please drop by my website, amyruttan.com, or give me a shout on Twitter @ruttanamy.

With warmest wishes,

Amy Ruttan

Born and raised just outside Toronto, Ontario, **Amy Ruttan** fled the big city to settle down with the country boy of her dreams. After the birth of her second child Amy was lucky enough to realise her lifelong dream of becoming a romance author. When she's not furiously typing away at her computer she's mum to three wonderful children who use her as a personal taxi and chef.

Visit the Author Profile page at millsandboon.co.uk for more titles.

This book is dedicated to Robin,
my partner in crime for this duet.
You were awesome, and I would
work with you again in a heartbeat.
I'm so glad we got to meet face to face *finally*!

For my friend Shay,
who is just as giving and admirable as my
heroine. You do so much and ask for nothing.
So glad we're friends.

And of course Laura, my editor extraordinaire,
who concocted this idea. Also for Tilda,
who always helps out with my AFS
and keywords and for stepping in
while the rest of us were in California.

PROLOGUE

"THAT HAS TO be the most monotonous lecturer that I've ever had the displeasure to listen to," Shay teased as she took a sip of her pineapple cocktail. She glanced over shyly at Dr. Dante Affini, who was attending the same conference on trauma simulation as her in Honolulu. She felt as if she was talking too loudly, which was something she always did in the presence of a man she found utterly attractive. And Dr. Dante Affini was all that and more. Just a few days with him and she was a lost woman. Add in the tropical setting and drinks…

It was a perfect paradise.

Shay had intended to throw herself completely into her work, as she always did, but on the first day of the conference she'd bumped into Italian surgeon Dr. Dante Affini looking perplexed. He hadn't known where to go and she'd helped him.

Since she'd let him know that she was attending the same presentations as him, they'd been inseparable. She didn't mind in the least. Dante was handsome, charming, intelligent and single.

She bit her lip, blood heating her cheeks. What was she doing? She didn't get involved with doctors, but with Dante it was hard not to.

He didn't look down his nose at her for being a nurse practitioner. Usually at these kind of conferences the nurses stuck together and the physicians stuck together. Except Dante seemed to be the exception. He'd turned down golfing, dinners and drinks with the other surgeons to accompany her. They'd attended the same lectures and seemed to agree on the same approaches to medicine.

Now the conference was winding up and it had been Dante's idea to get drinks.

She knew she shouldn't have accepted his invitation. It was not something she was used to doing, but this was sort of a work vacation and for once, Shay thought, why not?

Dante was charming, sexy, and she'd been so busy with her work for the last couple of years that maybe it was the perfect time to kick back and have some fun.

"*Sì*, that was most terrible." He shuddered and took a drink of his pineapple juice, then turned around, his dark eyes flickering out over the water. "It is a beautiful night."

Shay nodded. "The breeze is nice. It was sweltering in that room."

"Yes, it was most unpleasant." He waved his hand in a sweeping arc. "This, however, is paradise."

And he wasn't wrong. The sun was setting, like molten gold against the turquoise water. Palm trees swayed gently in the breeze and the sky was darkening. Soon it would be full of stars as the hotel where the conference was being held was off the beaten track. It was on the North Shore and there wasn't much else around it. No city, no noise and no distractions. It was heavenly.

"I wish I had more time to explore," Shay said wistfully. "I never traveled much until I joined the United World Wide Health Association, but that's for work and I don't get a lot of downtime on assignments. It's all about the work."

Dante shook his head. "That is no way to live life."

"Maybe not, but I love what I do."

He smiled at her, that charming, sexy, crooked smile she was getting used to seeing every day.

She was going to miss it when the conference was over.

"Of course, who am I to talk about living life, *cara*? My main focus is also my work."

"See, then why harass me?" she teased.

"Still, when you take an assignment somewhere, you must have time off."

Shay shrugged. "A little bit, but lately my assignments have been to mainly Third World countries after they've suffered a natural disaster and it really isn't safe to wander away from base camp to take in the sights."

Dante grinned. "Did I mention how incredibly brave you are, *cara*? I admire that about you."

Warmth flooded her cheeks. She could listen to Dante talk all night. He had such a dreamy Italian accent but spoke English so fluently.

"I just do my job," Shay said, brushing off the compliment, because she was proud of the work she did. It was a way to honor her mother, who should be alive still, if it weren't for Hurricane Katrina and the aftermath. The ill-effects of a poisoned house had prematurely taken the life of her mother, in the end.

It was at that moment that Shay knew what direction she had to take her life.

She'd worked hard to get where she was.

Now her job was to train other nurses and first responders by using simulation, so that they could go into the war zones, the disaster areas, and save lives, because that was all that mattered.

Saving lives.

"You do more than that, *cara*. I see it—you care about people and that's what makes you special." That smile disappeared and he fiddled with the straw in his drink. "Not everyone cares so much about others."

She was glad that the sun was setting, so that he couldn't see the blush he was causing.

Dante affected her in a way no man had in a long time. She was nervous around him. Giddy.

If she were anywhere else, she'd distance herself from him, but because she'd never see him again she figured it was okay to engage in harmless flirtation.

In a fantasy.

Not that anything would happen between the two of them.

Says who?

"Thank you," she finally said, trying to shake out the naughty thoughts suddenly traipsing across her mind.

"So let's do something about your lack of exploring," Dante said, setting down his empty glass on the bar. "Come."

"What?" she asked, confused.

"Look, it's our last night in paradise. Let's walk down to the beach and take a walk through the waves, follow the shore. It's a beautiful night."

"I don't know…"

What're you waiting for?

She glanced up at Dante, who stood in front of her, those dark eyes twinkling in the waning sunlight, the breeze making his short mop of ebony curls stir. His white cotton shirt billowed, so she could see the outline of his hard, muscular chest. His bronzed skin glowing in the waning light and, of course, that lopsided smile.

"What about the *luau*? Aren't we supposed to go there and network? You've traveled so far to attend this, don't you want to mingle?"

He snorted. "I have done enough networking to last a lifetime. For once I've no desire to talk about medicine. Tonight is a beautiful night. Let's go."

Go.

"Okay," Shay said, not needing any more convincing. She finished her drink and set her empty glass down on the bar and took his hand. It was strong and she was surprised how easily her hand slipped into his. She hoped he didn't notice that her nails were much too short, that her palms were rough from the hard physical work. She envied well-manicured nails, perfectly coifed hair, women who had time for makeup and clothes that weren't torn, stained or scrubs.

Only Dante didn't seem to care.

She couldn't believe that he'd chosen to spend all his free time with her this week.

A surgeon and a nurse.

Don't worry about that now. Just enjoy it. Live the fantasy for one night.

They walked away from the bar, down a winding sandy path to the beach. It was tranquil and a bit deserted at the moment. It was perfect.

"Hold on," she said. She let go of Dante's hand.

"What're you doing?" he asked.

"Taking off my shoes. The sand is getting in and I hate that feeling of sand in your shoes."

He chuckled. "Good idea."

They kicked off their shoes and carried them as they headed down to the shore. The sun was almost gone, as if it were disappearing behind a curtain of water. It was picture-perfect. The water licked at their toes as they walked in silence along the shoreline.

It was the perfect end to the conference.

Tomorrow she'd be flying back to New Orleans for a short time and then off on her next assignment to the Middle East. Always moving, as she'd been doing her whole life. No stability. No roots. New Orleans was just a base for her, but it really wasn't home since her mother died and she didn't know why she kept returning to it.

"You seem sad all of a sudden, *cara.*"

The way he called her *cara* made her tremble with anticipation.

"I was just thinking how wonderful this week has been." She bit her lip and sighed. "It's been amazing getting to know you, Dante."

He smiled and then ran his knuckles across her cheek. "I've enjoyed my time with you as well, *cara.*"

Shay's pulse began to race and she closed her eyes, his touch making her heart skip a beat, and then, before she had a chance to say anything else, his lips claimed hers.

She dropped her shoes to the sand and sank into the kiss, wrapping her arms around him and pulling him close.

Dante's kiss deepened, his tongue pushing past her lips; it was a kiss that seared her soul.

"Shay," he whispered, his mouth still close to her, his hands cupping her face. "I'm sorry, I couldn't help myself. You're so beautiful, so wonderful…" He kissed her again.

"I don't want this to end," she whispered against his ear as he held her close, his hands drifting down her back.

"Me neither."

"Then let's not let tonight end." She took his hand. "Let's go to your room…"

"Are you sure, *cara*?" he asked.

"Positive. We can just have tonight. I'm not looking for anything long-term, Dante."

Just passion. Unforgettable passion.

That was what she craved right now.

He smiled. "I want tonight too."

Dante took her hand and they picked up their shoes and headed back to the hotel, to his room and something wonderful that she'd always remember…

Dante didn't know what he was thinking when he bent down to kiss Shay, other than that the need to connect with her was so totally overwhelming. With the tropical wind blowing wisps of her honey-blonde hair around her heart-shaped face, he couldn't resist her siren call.

He didn't know what possessed him, other than absolute desire and need, because he'd sworn when Olivia broke his heart he'd keep away from women. Love was a loss of control and he hated losing that loss of control.

Only from the moment he'd met Shay, when she'd reached out to help him, he couldn't help himself. He knew he should've stayed away, but couldn't. Her brown eyes were warm, friendly, and the more he got to know her, the more he felt completely at ease with her.

To the point where his carefully constructed walls came down.

"*Cara*, I want you so bad," he whispered against her neck.

"I want you too," she said, her breath hot against his skin. It drove him wild.

It's only for one night.

And he had to keep reminding himself of that. That it was only one night.

She only wants tonight. I can give her tonight.

His heart didn't have to get hurt.

You don't have one-night stands, a little voice

reminded him, but he shook that thought away. His brother did and he fared just fine. Dante was not his father. He wasn't married, he wasn't hurting anyone, they were both consenting adults.

This was what his younger brother, Enzo, lived by; he could do that too, if only for one night.

Shay sighed as he ran his fingers through her silky hair as she wrapped her arms around him. Her long, delicate fingers tickling at the nape of his neck.

Mio Dio. It was only for tonight.

He could give himself over to one night. One night didn't mean forever.

It couldn't.

CHAPTER ONE

DANTE CLENCHED HIS fists as he jammed them into the pockets of his crisp white lab coat. Everything about him was controlled and ordered. Only today his schedule was off, and he was not in the mood for meeting the practitioner from America and running a simulation lab with him. And it wasn't just for one day; he'd then have him working under him as a surgical nurse in his operating room for twelve weeks.

Twelve weeks might not seem long in the grand scheme of things, but if Dante and this nurse practitioner didn't get along, then twelve weeks would feel like an eternity.

He remembered the last American from the United World Wide Health Association he'd worked with two years ago and that had been a nightmare. She'd been totally unorganized and needed constant guidance, which had driven him crazy.

Not all Americans are bad.

And his mood lightened as he thought of Shay and that stolen night in Oahu. She was the first woman he'd been with since Olivia had crushed his heart. Shay was one American he could get used to having around. Even now, months later, he could still feel her lips on his.

Only she was off who knew where on her latest assignment and he had to make nice with a stranger. Someone he didn't trust, and it brought back why he was in a bad mood.

His father. Someone else he absolutely didn't trust.

At dinner last night with his younger brother, Enzo, Dante had learned that their father, Prince Marco Affini, had once again sold off more of the family land. And he was eyeing the land their late mother had left in trust for Dante and Enzo until they married and produced an heir. At least their father couldn't sell it off yet. Unless they married before they turned thirty-five and produced an heir within a year of that marriage. Last night Enzo had reminded Dante once again that soon Dante would be turning thirty-five in a matter of months, without a marriage in sight.

Dante was painfully aware that his villa on Lido di Venezia was in danger of being sold as well, because that had been his maternal grandfather's home.

The villa on the sandbar, a ten-minute ferry ride from Venice proper, was part of Dante's inheritance. It would be his as long as he married and produced an heir by the time he was thirty-five, according to the stipulations of the trust fund and the marriage contract between his parents, as his mother had been a commoner and his father of royal blood.

And his thirty-fifth birthday was approaching fast, without a wife or heir in sight.

And whose fault was that?

It was his. He knew it; he just didn't have any desire to get married after what had happened with his ex, Olivia, and he didn't want to have a child out of wedlock. Even if he did, that wouldn't help him recover his inheritance, such were the archaic terms of the trust.

If he didn't get married and have a child, he would lose his home, everything that was meant for him by his late mother, including his beloved vineyard in Tuscany.

His grandfather had worked that vineyard. It was his pride and joy. Even though the family had money, his maternal grandfather always took pride in working his land. A work ethic that Dante had picked up on. He loved saving lives and he loved the life that bloomed in his vineyard in Tuscany.

Dante loved it there.

He loved working the land himself as well and the thought of someone else owning it was too much to bear.

It kept him awake most nights and he had the legal receipts to prove that he'd tried to get around the trust his mother signed on her wedding day, but it was ironclad. His father had the upper hand, until Dante and Enzo were married.

Dante downed the shot of espresso he'd grabbed before he headed to the lecture hall where he'd welcome the new United World Wide Health Association nurses and first responders who had come from all over Italy to join the organization. Here they'd learn what they needed to know, and then they would disperse over the world, providing health care.

Dante admired them and, even though he didn't want to be here and meet with his new associate from the United States, he knew he couldn't take his frustrations out on them.

He took a deep breath, ran his hand through his

dark hair as he glanced in a mirror briefly, cursing inwardly for not having shaved the stubble from his face, and he hated the dark circles under his eyes, but he hadn't got much sleep last night.

Once, he'd had the chance to save all the land meant for him, but that had cost him his heart and he swore he would never fall into that trap again. He just had to get used to the fact he was going to lose it all.

He was going to let down his brother and the memory of his mother.

His father would sell it all off and Dante would have to find a new place to live in a matter of a few months. He shook his head as he tried not to think about that now. He had to be charming and affable as the head of trauma at the Ospedale San Pietro.

Bracing himself now, Dante opened the door, ready to greet the American.

"*Ciao*, I'm Dr. Dante Affini, Head of..."

The nurse turned, just slightly, and Dante couldn't believe who he was looking at. His pulse raced and a rare smile tugged at the corner of his mouth. It was Shay!

She looked stunning. She was absolutely glowing, her cheeks rosy with a bloom she didn't have before.

Her honey-blonde hair wasn't as long as he remembered. She'd cut it, shorter in a bob, but it suited her delicate heart-shaped face. Those dark brown eyes of hers were warm and welcoming as she smiled at him, her pink lips soft and inviting. He could still feel them pressed against his. A blush rose in her round, creamy cheeks, deepening the healthy glow. Her lithe frame was fuller, but the curves suited her. "Hello, Dante."

"Shay?" Dante whispered, and then he smiled, realizing it was her who was here to work with him. "What are you doing here? I thought... I thought Daniel Lucey was going to be running this program."

"He was," Shay said. "But something came up for him, so I jumped at the chance to come to Italy and take an easier job for a while."

"An easier job? You're never one to back away from a challenge, *cara*."

A pink blush deepened on her cheeks and she tucked away an errant silky strand behind her ear. "I know, but I have no choice." She bit her lip. "Dante, I took this job because…because I'm pregnant."

Pregnant. Shay was having a baby?

It hit him and for a moment he wasn't sure he'd heard her correctly. Well, that explained the glow and the newly acquired curves. And then another realization struck him…

"Is it… Is it mine?"

"Yes." She bit her lip in a way that had driven him wild before but now filled him with a sense of trepidation.

A baby.

He had put up the walls to protect himself for a reason and he'd been a fool for letting her in back in Oahu.

It had been a moment of complete weakness on his part.

Dante scrubbed a hand over his face.

Why didn't she tell me? Was he really the father? Olivia had led him to believe that she carried his baby, only then he'd found out she'd tricked him. She'd already been pregnant when they'd slept together. Olivia had viewed Dante as perfect daddy material for another man's child…

He was angry. Angry at himself for thinking Shay might be different, but apparently not. He should've known better—a week and a one-night stand were no time to get to know someone. To trust someone.

A pink blush tinged her creamy cheeks. "I took this job so that I could tell you in person."

"Why didn't you tell me sooner?" he demanded. "Why didn't you contact me before you showed up here? As soon as you found out? It's been months, Shay. You can understand my trepidation. My anger, surely?"

She winced. "I know. But I've only very recently found out myself, Dante. I'm sixteen weeks."

"Four months in and you expect me to believe that you just found out?" Dante scoffed.

"Yes. I was working in a war-torn area. My periods have always been irregular and I put their absence down to stress and travel. I wasn't keeping that close an eye on dates, but something told me that it had been too long. I took a test, which came out positive, but then there was no way to contact you. Communication was spotty."

Dante saw red. "You were pregnant in a war zone?"

Her eyes narrowed. "There are lots of pregnant women in war zones."

Dante cursed under his breath and scrubbed a hand over his face. "That's not what I meant."

"Sure sounded like it." She crossed her arms and he noticed her breasts were fuller and he recalled at that moment the way his hands fit so nicely around them.

Get control of yourself.

"Fine. So you couldn't get word to me."

"No, I thought it would be news better delivered in person."

"I want a paternity test," he demanded.

Shocked and hurt, Shay glared at him. "It's your baby, Dante. I haven't been with anyone else."

"You didn't even know you were pregnant right away, so you understand my hesitancy. We used protection," he said.

"A faulty condom. They're not infallible." Shay sighed. "And I don't sleep around. I don't sleep with strangers."

"Wasn't I a stranger, *cara*?"

She shot him daggers. "I didn't come here to make you a father, Dante. I actually took the job because it paid well, so that I could take a longer maternity leave when I return to the States."

"So you considered not telling me?"

"Of course not. You have the right to know about your child, Dante. What I'm saying is that I don't expect anything from you."

Everything was sinking in and he was having a hard time processing for a moment. He wanted to believe that she was telling him the truth, but he'd been burned before. And thanks to his father's indiscretions the entire world seemed to know that he was a prince, poised to inherit a vast estate of land and money. Wasn't that what had drawn Olivia to him?

Of course, if Shay was pregnant with his child, it solved all of his problems.

He had to be married and have an heir by the time he was thirty-five. There was nothing in the will that stated he had to stay married. And while Olivia had made him very wary of marriage, he had wanted to be a father for as long as he could remember. He wanted the happy family he'd never had growing up. Plus, he knew that Shay was passionate about her job. She wouldn't want to settle down in Italy with him—hadn't she told him that she feared staying in one place for too long? What if he could get full custody of the baby? Have the child he'd always wanted without risking his heart.

"Dante, say something. Anything," Shay said. "I know this must be a terrible shock."

Before he could say anything there was a knock on his door. His assistant poked her head round it. "Dr. Affini? The trainees are gathered in the lecture theatre and are waiting for you."

Dante acknowledged the woman before he turned back to Shay. "We'll talk later. We have a job to do."

Shay smiled, relieved. "Yes. We have a job to do."

He'd let her have relief for now, but this was far from over.

Shay had wanted to tell Dante that she was pregnant from the moment she'd found out. She was frustrated when she realized she'd put their child in danger, and then when he'd insinuated that, she'd felt even guiltier. She wasn't irresponsible. Once she'd known she was expecting, she'd been flown out, leaving her free to take over this assignment from her colleague Daniel, who'd sadly just been diagnosed with stage two colon cancer. She'd dreaded telling Dante here, at work, but she respected him and he deserved to know about their child. She also wanted him to know that she didn't expect anything.

She wasn't looking for a marriage or even for him to be part of the child's life if he didn't want to be.

She knew firsthand what it was like when a man was forced into staying.

Her own father had made that painfully clear to her until the day he'd left her and her mother.

So she knew what it was like to be rejected by her father and she didn't want that for her child. And that was why she'd been terrified of telling Dante. Terrified he'd reject her and the baby, which would make the next twelve weeks working with him miserable.

Glad to be able to focus for the moment on the job at hand, Shay took the time it took them to make their way to the lecture theatre to chat about the assignment with Dante.

"I think I'm pretty much up-to-date on what Daniel was planning to do and how he was going to implement the simulation and training program," Shay said as she skimmed through the binder that she'd been given as she'd boarded the plane.

"So, what happened to Daniel?" Dante asked.

"Cancer," Shay said sadly.

"That's too bad. I wish him a speedy recovery, but I wish they had told me he wasn't coming." Dante rubbed his dimpled chin, and those butterflies that liked to dance around in the pit of her stomach months ago were starting up again. She'd forgotten how he affected her. He was still so handsome, the stubble on his chin suited him and she resisted the urge to tuck back the errant strand of his thick black hair.

"I thought you had been informed that Daniel was no longer coming," she said.

"Clearly not," he snapped.

"Dante, you're clearly not okay with this."

"I'm fine," he said, and he took the binder from her, not even looking at her.

She knew he wasn't. This was not the same man she'd spent a fairy-tale week with in Oahu. Then again, she hadn't really been herself either. Like when she'd decided to throw caution to the wind and have a one-night stand.

"Okay, you're fine, then. Shall we go and talk to the trainees? They are waiting."

"Of course." Dante didn't even look at Shay as he opened the door on the far side of the room. It was as if he was angry that she was here.

Can you blame him?

They walked out onto the stage of the small lecture theatre. The first two rows were filled with new United World Wide Health Association recruits, men and women who would be taking a crash course in first response and trauma.

Dante's job was to teach them trauma surgery and Shay was going to run them through a course of simulations. Based on situations she'd found herself in when she'd first started with the United World Wide Health Association.

She kind of envied all those hopeful faces, the thirty-odd new recruits. Her first days in the UWWHA working the field were some of her favorite times. Before she took this assignment she'd been going to take a field job in the Middle East to help vaccinate refugees.

Only that was before she'd found out she was pregnant. She couldn't go then and had been weighing up her options, and then this position had become available. The more romantically minded would probably call it fate.

This would be her last foreign assignment for a long time and she was going to make the most of it.

Her career and her unborn child mattered

to her. She was going to make sure her son or daughter had a good life and this job in Venice would give her a strong foundation. Even if she had to give up on her dreams for now.

The recruits were from all over Italy and some from Switzerland and France. They could all speak English and French, which Shay understood, and she was glad when Dante started to speak French to them over Italian, which she was still trying to pick up.

If her news had shaken him before, Dante didn't show it now as he spoke highly of the United World Wide Health Association and the twelve-week training program they would be completing at the hospital under his and Shay's guidance.

A baby hadn't been in her plans either, but it had happened and she was going to be a good mother and continue with her career. Even if it was going in a slightly different direction than she'd thought. She wouldn't pine away after a man who didn't want her as her mother had done.

"Your dad'll come back, Shay. You'll see. I'm his wife. He went to Alaska to work for the crab season. He'll be back and he'll take us all up to Alaska."

Of course, he never did come back.

He was still alive, the last Shay heard, but didn't want anything to do with her.

He'd moved on and he certainly didn't care that their house had been destroyed by Katrina and that his wife had died soon after from mold poisoning.

"Shay Labadie will explain the simulation scenarios you'll be going through." Dante stepped away from the podium and Shay shook the thoughts of her father from her head.

She was here to do a job.

And she always did a good job. Always saw a position through to the end, no matter what life threw at her.

She got up and explained the simulations that she would be running them through and answered questions. When she was done, the director of the UWWHA took the podium and she went and stood beside Dante. There was tension pouring off him and he barely looked at her.

Not that she could blame him.

She had dropped the fact that he was going to be a father on his lap.

She would've been more surprised if he weren't shocked by the prospect.

Once the director finished talking, there was a mix and mingle session, so that everyone could get to know one another. Shay walked toward the stairs at the end of the stage, but Dante grabbed her arm, holding her back.

"A moment *per favore*, Shay." He pinched the bridge of his nose and sighed. "First, I was serious when I said I would like a paternity test done."

"Okay." He'd been right when he'd reminded her that they were strangers who'd slept together, much as it smarted that her word wasn't enough to convince him that she didn't sleep around. "Anything else?"

"This is hard for me to say."

"Dante, you don't have to do anything. I already told you that I'm not asking for anything."

"I know you're not," he said quickly. "I am."

"What… I… You're what?" Shay didn't know how to take that response. Now she was shocked, so she asked cautiously, "What're you asking for?"

"Not much. Just that if the paternity test proves that I'm the father—"

"Which it will," she interrupted.

"*If* it does," he said through clenched teeth, "I want you to marry me."

Of all the things she'd thought he'd say, that wasn't one of them.

She hadn't been expecting that.

CHAPTER TWO

"YOU WANT…WHAT?" Shay was trying to process what Dante had said and she wasn't sure that she completely understood him. "Could you repeat that?"

"I said that if the paternity test proves I'm the father I want you to marry me." There was no smile on his face, no glint in his eye letting her know that he was joking, because he had to be joking, right? Men just didn't ask women they'd slept with once to marry them, did they?

"That's what I thought you said, but then I was thinking that there was no way you could be asking me that." She tried to move past him, because this was a bit crazy. This was not the Dante she remembered, the Dante she knew.

You don't know Dante, remember?

And she didn't. Usually she knew the men she slept with a bit better, but when she'd been in Oahu she'd thrown caution to the wind when she'd succumbed to Dante's kiss.

Even now, standing here in front of him, she had a hard time trying to forget the way his arms had felt around her. The way he'd whispered *cara* in her ear.

This reaction to him is why you're pregnant in the first place.

"Well, I'm not asking you," he said.

"You're crazy." She tried to leave.

He stepped in front of her to block her. "I'm not asking you, Shay. I'm telling you. If I'm the father, we will get married."

What?

"You're telling me?" She cleared her throat. "Seriously?"

Dante nodded. "Yes. You will marry me."

Shay tried not to laugh at the absurdity of it. This was not real life.

"And what about the paternity test you're so adamant I take?"

He glared at her. "I only want marriage if the test proves I'm the father."

"And if it doesn't?" Which was absurd. She hadn't been with anyone since him, and before him there'd been no one else for a long time.

"Won't it?"

She crossed her arms, glaring at him. Suddenly

she was having a hard time finding him charming. Sexy, yes, but charming—heck, no. More annoying than anything.

"You're the father," she replied icily.

"Then you will marry me once we receive the results."

She snorted. "How romantic."

"Nothing about this is romantic, *cara*." The endearment he used on her, his voice still deep and rich. She could hear that whisper in her ears: *cara*.

"Do you love me?" she asked point-blank, shaking those thoughts from her head.

He cocked his eyebrows. "This has nothing to do with love."

"So the answer is no," she said.

"Were you expecting me to say yes? Other than one week together, we don't know each other."

"Exactly, so why would I marry you?"

He frowned. "To give our child legitimacy. A stable home. The guarantee that it will have two parents. This is a business arrangement for the sake of the child."

The premise of giving her child a good home life was very tempting, but she knew how this played out. She'd been that child after all and she wouldn't put her child through that. Through the resentment, bitterness and heartache. To the point that her father had walked away and didn't even want to see her again.

No, she didn't want that for her baby.

She didn't want her baby to feel that pain. Only he seemed to really want this baby and her father had never wanted her.

Another parent involved, especially a stationary one, means you can pursue assignments anywhere in the world.

"I'm not going to marry you," she said. "I'm here to work." She tried to leave the room, but he stepped in front of her, grabbing her by the arm, his dark eyes blazing.

"I don't think you know what you're talking about."

"I think I do," she snapped, shrugging her arm out of his grip.

"So I'm not to have access to my child?" he demanded.

"I never said that."

"You won't marry me. So that means I won't see this child. You're only in Italy for twelve weeks. Then what happens? You won't even be here when our child is born."

"Dante, I'm not denying you access to your child. I want you to be part of his or her life. We don't have to get married to raise this child. We don't even need to live in the same country."

He opened his mouth to say more when his pager buzzed. He looked down. "Incoming trauma, *dannazione*. This conversation isn't over." He stormed out of the room, his white lab coat billowing out behind him from his long strides. He was a force of nature to be reckoned with.

Shay breathed an inward sigh of relief, because for now she was able to get a breather, but she knew that this was probably far from over.

Dante stuck his head back into the room. "Are you coming, Shay? There is incoming trauma and you're to be my nurse for the next twelve weeks. I need you by my side."

By his side.

Only she wasn't sure she was going to survive the next twelve weeks. By the way things were going she was either going to kill him or fall in love with him.

And succumbing to the passion, the desire, she felt for him was not an option. Neither was falling in love.

She had to guard her heart.

Shay was not her mother and wouldn't be easily persuaded by loving a man. This was *her* life and she was going to live by her own wit.

"Of course."

She shook her head; she had to get back in the game and focus on her work here. This was her job and, when she'd found out that she was pregnant after one night of forbidden passion, she'd sworn that she wasn't going to let the pregnancy interfere with her job performance. She was a damn good nurse practitioner and simulation trainer. And that wasn't going to change.

Even though she was starting to blossom and her center of gravity was shifting, she was able to keep up with Dante's quick pace as they navigated the hallways through the hospital. He finally slowed down when they entered the trauma ward, where there was a flurry of activity. Shay could see water ambulances outside a set of automatic doors, where they were bringing in stretchers of patients.

"What happened?" Dante asked in Italian, that much she understood. The man spoke quickly and then pointed to where Dante was needed.

"Shay, this way," Dante called, waving his hand and directing her to follow him.

They entered a private treatment bay, where a man lay seriously wounded.

"He's American. Your presence might calm him," Dante whispered.

Shay nodded. "What happened?"

"A *vaporetto* was tossed when a large cruise ship came into the lagoon. The cruise ship sent a wave into St. Mark's Square and there were some injuries there as well."

"Vaporetto?" Shay asked as she pulled on a trauma gown and gloves.

"Water taxi," Dante said as he pulled on his own gloves. "This has been happening more and more. Especially during the summer months, when the tourists flock the city. Too much traffic." He shook his head with disgust.

Shay nodded and headed over to the patient, who was conscious and had a mask on. His brown eyes were wide with fear as he looked around the room.

"I can't understand a word," he mumbled through the oxygen mask.

"Me neither," Shay said gently. "I'm learning, though."

"You're American?" he asked, a hint of relief in his voice.

"I am. I'm a nurse practitioner with the United World Wide Health Association. Can you tell me what happened?"

"I don't know, I don't remember. One moment my wife and I were taking a water taxi from Lido di Venezia to St. Mark's, and then the next thing I know we're in the water. Oh, goodness, where is my wife?"

"What is her name?" Shay asked.

"Jennifer Sanders."

"I'll find her for you in a moment," Shay said gently. "It's important we make sure you're okay first."

"I can't move. I can't feel my legs," the man said, his voice rising in panic.

Dante shot her a concerned look. "What is your name, *signor*?"

The man looked at Dante. "Are you the doctor?"

"*Sì*. Can you tell me your name?"

"James, but my friends call me Jim."

Dante smiled at him. "I'm going to examine your abdomen. Tell me if anything hurts, and then we'll get an MRI of your spine."

The man nodded. Shay lifted his shirt and there was dark bruising; his belly was distended, which was a sign there was internal bleeding. The bleeding would have to be stopped before they could worry about his back. In this case internal bleeding trumped paralysis.

The man cried out when Dante did a palpation over his spleen.

"We need to get a CT scan of his abdomen, see how bad the bleeding is," Dante whispered to Shay.

"Where do I go to order that?" she asked.

"I will. You stay with him. Prep him for the procedures." Dante left the room.

Shay calmed their patient down and got an IV started, drawing the blood work needed before surgery. She had no doubt that with extensive bruising and pain Jim would need surgery and fast.

"What's your name?" Jim asked.

"Shay Labadie," she said as she took his vitals, writing them down.

"Baton Rouge?" he asked.

"No, close, though. New Orleans proper." She smiled.

"I thought it was a Louisiana accent. I'm from Mississippi. Picayune to be exact."

"Not far, then." She smiled at him warmly, trying to reassure him as his blood pressure was rising.

He grinned faintly as his eyes rolled back into his head and the monitors went into alarm.

"I need a crash cart!" she shouted, slamming her hand against the code blue button as the rest of the team in the room jumped into action. Some situations transcended the language barrier.

"Nurse Labadie, if you contact Dr. Prescarrie, he is the neurologist. He'll be able to determine the extent of the nerve damage in our patient." Dante wanted to keep Shay busy, keep her away from the OR table, but she didn't budge. She stood by his side, passing him the instruments he needed without him having to ask for them.

She knew exactly what he needed and when.

And she was so calm about it. That was what bothered him the most. As if nothing fazed her.

She was good at her job.

Though he shouldn't be surprised. He'd been impressed by her when they were in Oahu together at the conference. Only he hadn't got to see her actually work. Now he had that privilege, but he was also very aware of the fact that she was pregnant.

With his child.

Maybe your child.

He was still reeling over the realization Shay was here and pregnant with his child as he removed Mr. Sanders's badly damaged spleen.

"I will contact him, but does he speak English?" she asked.

"He speaks French and I know that you can speak that. I heard you speak that before."

"Okay, I'll have him paged once Mr. Sanders is stable." She handed him a cautery that he didn't ask for, but damn if he didn't need it right at that moment.

"Grazie," he said grudgingly.

"You seem tense, Dr. Affini," Shay remarked.

"Of course I'm tense. I have a man open on the table."

And you've just walked back into my life carrying my baby.

Her presence here totally threw his controlled world off balance. Thoughts of Shay were kept to the privacy of his memories. To the nights he was alone and lonely, wishing he could have more than he was allotted in life. That was when he thought of Shay and their time together.

He'd romanticized her. The one stolen moment

he could treasure forever and now she was here and he wasn't sure how to handle it.

Her presence unnerved him completely.

"Is there anything I can do to ease your tension?" she asked. "I mean, if my job as a scrub nurse isn't up to scratch..."

"It's fine. There is nothing you can do. Well, there is one thing, but you refused." He quickly glanced over at her and he could see her brow furrow above that surgical mask.

"This is not the time to discuss it." There was a hint of warning in her voice.

Dante raised his eyebrows. He'd never heard Shay speak in that tone before. Even at the conference when there were idiots either hitting on her or talking over her, because she was *just a nurse*, she'd always smiled sweetly and taken them down a peg. This was something different.

A clear warning.

"Why not? I like chatting while I work." He didn't, but he liked getting under her skin the way she got under his.

She snorted. "You didn't seem very receptive to talking before."

"It depends what the subject is," he teased.

"Well, I can say in no uncertain terms the subject you want to discuss, Dr. Affini, is off-limits."

He chuckled but didn't say anything further to her as he completed the splenectomy and stabilized the patient. Once he was done, Shay walked away from him and he could see her on the operating theatre's phone, obviously paging Dr. Prescarrie about Mr. Sanders's spinal injuries.

Not only was he impressed by her skill in a surgical situation, but he admired her strength. Women in his circles usually would balk under interrogation. Of course, women in his circles, women like Olivia, wouldn't even be in an operating theatre, getting their hands dirty.

"What you do is noble, Dante. It's just that I don't want to hear about it. Can't you just keep that to yourself?"

"And what am I supposed to talk about, Olivia? Fashion, cars?"

"The vineyards and, yes, it wouldn't hurt you to immerse yourself in the world of privilege you were born into."

Dante snorted as he pulled off his gloves and gown, disposing of them.

Olivia had hated that he was a trauma surgeon, working in a public hospital rather than in a private clinic. And his choice of surgery. Why couldn't he do something like plastic surgery?

In her mind, a prince who was a surgeon needed to do something glamorous that dealt with the glitterati, not just anybody who stumbled in through the doors.

Only that wasn't him. That was his father's world and he loathed it.

Dante might be a prince, poised to inherit a large vineyard in Tuscany and his villa on the Lido di Venezia, as well as a hefty sum of money, but Prince was just a title. It wasn't as if he were a member of the British royal family set to inherit the throne.

Being a prince was just a status in Italy. Nothing more.

His work as a surgeon meant so much more to him.

Working with his hands, doing something important whether it was tending the vines as his grandfather so lovingly had or saving a life.

That was what mattered to him.

Just like the baby that Shay was carrying inside her.

If it's yours.

Even though there was no long-term future for

Shay and him, he was determined to be a good father if she would just let him.

"Dr. Prescarrie should be down soon," Shay remarked, coming into the scrub room. "He insisted on his own scrub nurse, though."

"As well he should," Dante said as he washed his hands. "You're on my service."

Shay rolled her neck and winced.

"Are you well?" he asked, concerned, seeing the discomfort etched on her face.

"Yes, just tired. I'm still getting used to the time change. A bit jet-lagged still."

"Why don't you go home and rest?"

She frowned. "I'm fine. I can still work and my shift isn't over yet."

"Shay, you need to take care of yourself. You're possibly carrying my baby."

There was a gasp behind them and they both spun around to see another nurse standing there, her brown eyes wide with shock as she looked between them.

"*Sì?*" Dante asked in exasperation and frustration. He had no doubt that the nurse had overheard.

"*Siamo spiacenti, il Principe, non volevo interromperla.*" She was apologizing for interrupting them, but Mrs. Sanders was being treated for a broken wrist and was inquiring after her husband. The patient was worried. Dante told the nurse that he would be there shortly to speak to her.

The nurse nodded and left.

Shay was standing there just as stunned. "She just called you *il Principe*. Why did she refer to you as the Prince?"

Dante sighed. This was what he'd wanted to avoid.

It was a title and a burden to him.

He was Dante and nothing more.

"Because I am," Dante said.

"You're a prince? A real prince?"

"Sì..." Dante sighed. "I am, so your child will also inherit my title if the child is mine. You may be carrying a royal baby."

"Shay!"

Shay just shook her head and kept walking. She was trying to process what Dante had said to her: that her child was going to have a royal title. Only *if* the baby was his and that annoyed her even more. He was so suspicious of her. She hadn't known that he was a prince, so he couldn't accuse her of fortune hunting.

But maybe that's why he's so suspicious of paternity?

This was all just too surreal.

Of course, it was only fitting that he drop a bombshell on her, just as she'd done to him.

"Shay!"

She stopped and sighed. She couldn't act like this. This was not professional and she'd promised herself that she would be above all professional when dealing with Dante. She was an adult and this was their child.

"I'm sorry, Dante," she said. "I guess it was a bit of a shock to find out who you are."

"It doesn't change who I am, though," he said gently.

"How would I know that? I barely know you." She shook her head. "We're strangers."

He sighed at that. "This is true. One week at a conference means nothing."

"I do realize we have to get to know each other if we're both going to be involved in this child's life."

"*Sì*, I agree. Which is why you will marry me if the test is positive."

Shay rolled her eyes. "Not this again. I'm not marrying you, Dante. I'm not going to marry someone I don't love."

"I'm not talking about a marriage of love," he said matter-of-factly. "I'm talking about a marriage of convenience. Just for a year. You live under my roof and we pretend to be man and wife in public."

"Dante, I'm only here for twelve weeks."

"So? You're going on maternity leave when you get back to the United States, *sì*?"

"Yes, but… I have to go back to the States. My work visa is only good for twelve weeks."

"If we marry, then you won't need a visa. You say it's my child, so why not have *our* child here, in my country?"

"I… I can't—I won't—give up my life, Dante."

"After a year is over, then you can walk away. With our child, as long as I have parental rights. I will continue to financially support the child."

"What do you gain from this?" she asked, confused. It all seemed too easy.

"An heir." He dragged his hand through his dark hair. "I will support the child either way, but while you're here in Italy, under my roof, I can protect you. Care for you."

She bit her lip, mulling it over, but she didn't want to marry. Ever.

Unless it was for love. Absolute, head-over-heels, can't-get-enough-of-each-other love. She let a hand drift over her belly.

"I can't, Dante," she said.

He frowned. "You're confused. Of course you are. I can see it. You should know that the baby won't inherit any of my family land if he or she is not legitimized."

"Is that a bad thing?" Shay asked. "Perhaps it's better for our baby to be away from all of that."

His eyes narrowed. "I take my family history very seriously. Being an Affini heir is a thing of pride."

And then she felt bad because she was insulting him. His values.

Dante was not American. He came from a completely different world than she did.

How can you have family pride when you know nothing about the name you were born with?

Still, she couldn't agree to marry him. Not now. She needed time to think and she wanted to talk to her friend and colleague, Aubrey, about it. She was so confused.

"We should go and talk to Mrs. Sanders. I'm

sure she's worried." She turned and kept walking toward the room where Mrs. Sanders had got her broken wrist taken care of. Dante thankfully took the hint as he fell into step beside her.

Mrs. Sanders was lying in a bed, her wrist in a cast, and Shay could see the pain and worry etched on her face. She opened her eyes when they walked into the room.

"Please tell me you have word on my husband," Mrs. Sanders said.

"I'm Dr. Affini and I did the surgery on your husband."

"Were you told why he went to surgery?" Shay asked gently.

"He had internal bleeding?" Mrs. Sanders said, a hint of uncertainty in her voice. "That's all I know."

"Your husband had major lacerations to his spleen," Dante said gently. "I had to remove it."

Shay rubbed the patient's shoulder as she began to cry.

"He came through the splenectomy well," Dante said. "Dr. Prescarrie is our neurologist. He is going to check out your husband's spine."

"Why?" Mrs. Sanders asked, her eyes tracking to Shay and then back to Dante.

"He was complaining of loss of sensation before we took him into surgery," Dante said. "Dr. Prescarrie will be able to determine if the paralysis is temporary and what damage was done to the spine. We take loss of function very seriously."

"Oh, no. This is our thirtieth anniversary. Our kids surprised us with this trip to Italy. We're on a tour, you see…"

"Were you with the tour company when it happened?" Shay asked.

Mrs. Sanders shook her head. "No, we were having some free time in Venice. We're leaving for Tuscany tomorrow."

"Give me the number of the tour operator and I'll explain what happened. She can contact your family."

"It's in my purse over there." She inclined her head. "Thankfully, I wasn't thrown into the water. Our passports are in there too if you need them."

Shay smiled and brought Mrs. Sanders her purse, holding it open so the patient could pull out the information. Shay took it.

"I'll call the tour operator and they'll take care

of your belongings and everything," Shay said. "Don't you worry. Just rest."

Mrs. Sanders nodded and clutched her purse with her good arm.

"Dr. Prescarrie will update you on your husband as soon as possible, Signora Sanders. For now you'll stay in this room. Try to rest." Dante patted the patient's leg and they walked out of her room. Dante stopped at the nurses' station to give instructions to the staff about Mrs. Sanders's stay, before he headed back toward Shay.

"That was very good of you to say you'll call the tour company."

"Well, they're so far from home." Shay glanced down at the information in her hand. "Is there a place I can call from in private?"

"*Sì*, follow me." Dante held out his arm and led her to another part of the hospital until they were standing in front of an office. "This is my office and you may use the telephone in there to contact the tour operator."

He opened the door for her and flicked on the lights.

"Thank you, Dante."

He shrugged. "Take your time, but before you go I want to finish our conversation."

"I thought we *were* finished with that particular conversation."

A small smile twitched his lips. "No, we're not finished. Far from it. Besides, you have a test to go through, *cara*."

Dante shut the door and walked away, leaving Shay alone in his office. She breathed a sigh of relief as she took a seat in his leather office chair and punched in the number. She was connected right away to the tour operator and she explained the situation to them. Everything was worked out. Their room in Venice would be held for them for as long as they needed and the tour company would contact the emergency contacts in their file.

The tour company would also contact the insurance and everything would be taken care of.

Satisfied, Shay disconnected the call and leaned back in Dante's swivel chair. She closed her eyes and the baby fluttered around, feeling like a butterfly. Reminding her again that she was working a bit too hard.

The ob-gyn she'd seen in the United States had said she could do this work, but he had warned her to take it easy.

The only reason she had clearance to take this job was because it was less strenuous than the assignment she was originally on. Running a training and simulation program, as well as assisting a trauma surgeon in the operating theatre, should be a breeze.

The problem was, she hadn't taken a break.

Her blood sugar was dropping and she needed to eat something.

Something decent.

And she needed rest.

Dante might think their conversation wasn't over, but as far as she was concerned it was for the evening. She was going to head back to the villa she and her friend Danica were sharing, eat and get some sleep. Tomorrow was going to be a long day; she was going to run her first simulation.

She got up and found her way back to the small office she had been given on the other side of the hospital. She grabbed her purse and sweater. She headed toward the back door and from there it was a short walk to the house the United World Wide Health Association had rented for their staff.

If she had a moment, she'd talk to Dante again and tell him again that she wasn't going to marry him.

Convenience or not, she was a big girl and could take care of herself.

She didn't need his protection.

As she stepped outside she was blinded by flashing lights and a rush of people crowded her, pressing her back against the wall. She shielded her face, but she couldn't understand what they were asking her.

She caught a few words, like *prince* and *baby*.

Then there was a roar and string of loud, harsh words and strong arms came around her, pulling her close, and she realized it was Dante, shielding her. She clung to him as he shouted at the group of reporters and ushered her back inside. Once they were back inside and the shouting from the mob of reporters was drowned out, she sighed in relief.

"What in the world…?"

"The press got word that you might be carrying my heir," Dante snapped.

"*That's* what they were asking me?"

"*Sì,*" he said, his dark eyes twinkling with a

dangerous light, his hands on his hips, and he began to curse in Italian again.

"I thought that Italian princes were common?" Shay said, mimicking him. "I mean, not like the British royal family…"

"Yes, but with my family there is a bit more scandal. So my brother and I are often in the spotlight. We're favorites of the paparazzi."

"And I just gave them their latest scoop." She ran a hand over her belly. "Is this going to happen all the time?"

Dante scrubbed a hand over his face. *"Sì."*

"So that's what you meant by protecting me?" she asked.

He nodded curtly. "Where are you staying?"

"At the United World Wide Health Association house. It's not far from here."

He shook his head. "Not tonight, you're not. You're coming to my place."

"I am not!" she said, getting annoyed with him.

"You're going to cause a bigger scandal if you don't agree to my marriage suggestion, especially if the child is mine," Dante snapped. "You could ruin my reputation at this hospital."

Shay bit her lip. She didn't want to ruin his career or his reputation. "You want a marriage of convenience?"

"*Sì*, that way I can protect you. I have a restraining order against the paparazzi and it will protect you also, if you marry me."

"So just on paper we'll be married."

"*Sì*, but to make it look real you will have to move into my home for a year." He rolled his neck and tugged at the collar of his shirt, as if it were suffocating him. It clearly bothered him just as much as it bothered her.

"Do you have enough room?" Shay asked.

He chuckled. "I have an entire villa to myself on the Lido di Venezia. I can give you your own wing if you desire. Just say yes. Let me protect you and our child."

Even though she should say no, she didn't want paparazzi stopping her and accosting her when she moved around Venice. Especially where there was a language barrier. Dante could keep them at bay. She ran her hand over her belly again.

This was his baby too. Even if he didn't believe it at the moment.

What choice did she have? It was just for a year. Only she couldn't do it. She couldn't agree to the marriage.

"You're coming with me," Dante said. "We'll get the paternity test done now, put this doubt to rest."

"I don't have a say in this?"

"No, you don't."

And she had a feeling this was one of many arguments she was going to have with him over the course of the next twelve weeks. He'd won this round, but she'd win the next.

CHAPTER THREE

"YOU DID WHAT?"

Dante glanced into his office, where Shay was curled up on his sofa, sleeping. She was resting after the paternity test. Now they were waiting for the results and Dr. Tucci promised to rush them. Before they left, Dante was going to make sure that they were at least on their way to being man and wife, even if Shay kept saying no. He was still having a hard time trusting her, but deep down he felt as if this child was his. So he was going to make sure she married him. Then he could protect the trust his mother left and have something for his child. His child wouldn't have to worry about the future the way his father made Enzo and him so worried. Dante wouldn't sell off his child's inheritance just because he or she wasn't married by the time they were thirty-five. He wouldn't have such a foolish restriction.

Once he brought Shay back to his villa, the

press couldn't hound her. If she stayed by his side, she'd be safe as well.

There were still a few steps he had to take. Like convincing her to say yes and stay in Italy. *If* the child was his, he'd do the right thing to protect his child.

And if it's not?

He glanced at Shay sleeping so peacefully and he didn't even want to think of her betraying him the way Olivia had. His memory of Shay had been so pure and untainted.

The memory of their night together was the only thing besides the vineyard and surgery that made him happy. If she betrayed his trust like Olivia, that memory would be shattered. He'd have nothing pure to cling to when the loneliness gnawed at him.

"Dante, are you even listening to me?" Enzo asked on the other end of the phone.

"*Scusate*, it's been a trying day." He rubbed his temple where a tension headache was forming.

"I would say so," Enzo commiserated on the other end.

"I'm getting married. I just have to obtain a Nulla Osta as quickly as possible."

"She's not Italian?" Enzo asked.

"She's American."

"Why do you want to marry an American?"

"She's carrying my child."

"Are you sure?"

"*Sì*, I believe it is mine."

"You don't sound sure."

"The paternity test results will be ready soon." Dante sighed.

There was silence on the other end. "Dante, I know I have been bugging you to get married, but…did she even agree?"

"Not yet."

"Not yet?" Enzo asked.

"You don't have to say anything else," Dante said, cutting his brother off. He knew exactly where Enzo was going with this and he didn't want to be reminded about Olivia and the baby that wasn't his right now.

Shay was not Olivia.

"I don't want you to get hurt again," Enzo said gently. "It killed me to see you so hurt last time."

"I appreciate that, Enzo. However, if this is my baby, I will marry her."

"What if she's after your money? Your title? Even if the baby is yours, she could be just after the same things that Olivia was."

"She's not," Dante said. "She's already refused to marry me, remember? Several times. It's almost getting embarrassing now."

Enzo laughed. "Still…"

"No, there is no still. Shay's not after my money or anything. There will be ground rules to this marriage. It's just a marriage of convenience. Nothing more. She can continue to do her work, our baby will be protected and I will keep my inheritance. The trust Mother signed over to Father before she knew any better."

"What do you need from me?" Enzo asked.

"She's staying at our place."

"What do you mean?"

"Our childhood home, the one that was sold off before mother died and is now being rented to the United World Wide Health Association. She's staying there."

"Ah, so you want me to go collect her stuff?"

"Or at least tell someone there to collect it for her and then bring it to my place. That's where she'll be staying from now on. She was mobbed on her way out of the hospital this evening. The whole world will soon know about the Affini heir."

"I can't believe you did it, Dante. I can't believe you're going to get married and have an heir all within a year and so close to the cutoff date. You did it. You saved Grandfather's vineyard and Mamma's villa."

A smile crept across Dante's face as the reality sank in.

He had. He'd managed to keep a hold of all that was promised to him. All that money and land wouldn't pass back into their father's greedy hands. The land he loved so much, the vineyard, all of it would be saved. The relief that washed over him in that moment was almost palpable.

"Could you go and talk to her roommate as soon as possible?" Dante asked. "She's tired and I'm taking her back to my villa. She needs her rest."

"*Sì*, I'll go there as soon as I finish up at the clinic."

"*Grazie.*" Dante hung up the phone and then knelt beside Shay. She looked so peaceful sleeping, her face at ease, those long blond eyelashes brushing the tops of her round cheeks. He resisted the urge to reach out and run his thumb across those smooth, soft cheeks or to kiss her pink lips as he had back in Oahu.

The memory of which was still imprinted onto

his soul. And pregnancy just made her all the more beautiful.

She glowed.

Don't. Don't get attached. The results aren't in. Don't set yourself up for hurt.

"Shay," he said gently. "Wake up."

She roused. "Is something wrong?"

"It's time to leave. The paparazzi are still waiting out back, but I have a water taxi waiting for us to take us to Lido di Venezia. They won't follow us there."

"And the results of the test?"

"They'll be ready tomorrow morning. Come, stay at my place tonight, where I can keep you safe."

She nodded drowsily. He stood and helped her to her feet.

He guided her out of his office, down a winding staircase to the canal that bordered the hospital. The water-taxi operator helped Shay down into his boat and Dante followed.

It was dark out, but the city helped light the way. The hospital wasn't too far from the lagoon, but behind him he could hear the singing of the gondoliers, tempting tourists to take a ride. Shay settled against the back of the seat.

"I'm sorry, I can barely keep my eyes open." Her head was nodding.

"Put your head on my shoulder." He rested his arm against the back of the boat and she leaned into him. He could smell her perfume. Soft, feminine. Lilacs.

It reminded him of summers spent in Tuscany. Of the flowers blooming in his grandmother's garden, warmed by the hot sun. He couldn't help but smile. It was so right. It all seemed so right. Everything he wanted.

Be careful.

As they left the canals and headed out into the lagoon, there were stars in the sky. The city light drowned them out, but tonight the sky was clear enough you could make out a few. Ahead the Lido di Venezia was lit up with lights from restaurants and homes that littered the sandy shoal. Even farther away there were a couple of cruise ships and you could hear the music wafting from the upper decks.

It left a bad taste in his mouth.

Venice was becoming too much of a tourist trap.

Which was why he preferred Tuscany.

Sure, there were tourists, but there was more

space. And there were no tourists at his grandfather's vineyard.

My vineyard.

He glanced down at the small rounded swell
that Shay was instinctively cradling in her sleep.
That was his child. And even though he wasn't
sure, he reached out to touch it.

"Where are we?" Shay asked, waking with a
start. He pulled his hand back and moved his
arm.

"We're almost to my home. It's a short walk
from the pier to my villa."

"I'm sorry I fell asleep. I usually have more
stamina."

"You're pregnant. It's fine."

And it was more than fine.

For his family's legacy it was a lifesaver. And
for his heart, his longing for a child he'd thought
he'd never have, it was a dream come true.

As long as it's yours.

And that little naysaying voice slammed him
back to harsh reality. He was putting his heart
at risk again.

Dante climbed out of the water taxi first at the
docks and then held out his hand for Shay. Which

was good; she wasn't that sure-footed on boats anymore, since her center of gravity had shifted.

In some of the places she worked, boats were a way to get around, a way of life, so she was annoyed when Dante had to help her out of a modern, luxurious water taxi. It wasn't as if it were a skiff in the middle of a fast-flowing river in the South American jungle.

However, she'd forgotten how well her hand fit in his. How safe he made her feel, just like that night on the beach in Oahu. And she sighed; it slipped out unintentionally.

"What?" he asked as he helped her onto the pier.

"Nothing," she said, smiling up at him.

He smiled too and paid the water-taxi captain.

"Ciao," the captain said, waving at them as he puttered away out toward Venice. The moon was high in the sky, the dark water calm; only a few ripples from the water taxi disrupted the mirrorlike quality of the lagoon. It reminded her of nights in the French Quarter, by Jackson Square, and looking out over the Mississippi. Then there were the few scattered memories of her father taking her to Lake Pontchartrain to fish, before he left them. The moon would be so high over

the large lake and New Orleans out on the delta would glow and come to life.

It was all so perfect, this moment. But that was the thing. It was just a moment. Even when the results confirmed what she was saying, she couldn't believe he'd change his tune. He was so untrusting, so guarded, and she couldn't help but wonder why. Moments didn't last. She should know. Her father had proved that, and once her father had left, those nights had no longer been so perfect.

And this situation with Dante was far from perfect.

"Come," Dante said, interrupting her thoughts. "It's only a short walk to my villa."

They walked up the ramp from the dock onto the street.

Shay was surprised to see a few cars and a bus stop.

As if sensing her shock Dante chuckled. "There are no large canals here. Solid land here."

"I'm surprised you don't live in Venice."

He frowned. "I used to. I grew up there."

"Do your parents still live there?"

"No," he said tersely. "Our family home is no longer in our family."

"You sound annoyed by that."

"It's a long story," Dante said. "Besides, I prefer living here on the Lido di Venezia. It's peaceful here. There are tourists on the beach side, but I live on the lagoon side. I enjoy having a garden and trees. And most of the beaches at this end are private and owned by the hotels. Though to the south there are public beaches. The Adriatic is warm and very popular for young children. I spent many summers swimming here."

They turned down a small side street off the main street, the Gran Viale Santa Maria Elisabetta, not far from the lagoon, where residents could catch the ferries and *vaporetti*.

Shay was expecting a small home and was shocked when he opened a gate to a large, square villa that seemed to take up the entire block off the main street. At the top of the villa there looked to be a patio that would have views over the lagoon and to Venice.

"I shouldn't be surprised," she mumbled. "You are a prince, after all."

He grinned and pushed open the creaky iron gate. "This was my maternal grandparents' summer home—they were wealthy but not royalty. Unfortunately, it fell into disrepair."

"And you're putting it back together?"

He nodded quickly. "There are many rooms."

Dante unlocked the front door and led her inside. When he flicked on the light, Shay gasped at the beauty of a place so old. The stucco on the wall was painted in terra-cotta. The foyer was round like a turret, which you couldn't tell from the outside, which was square.

There were many arches leading off to various empty rooms.

"I haven't had much time," Dante said apologetically. "Just the kitchen has been renovated on this ground floor and the master suite, terrace and a couple of bathrooms on the next level."

She followed him past numerous rooms. There was a large room that looked as if it had a dining table and suspended over it was a beautiful glass chandelier, unlit as it hovered above the ghostly occupants.

"This is the kitchen. It backs onto the garden. You can't see much, but I have a couple of kiwi trees and an olive tree out there as well as a small pool." Dante flicked on another light, which illuminated a white, large and modern kitchen. "Are you hungry?"

"Yes," Shay admitted.

He smiled. "I thought as much. You need to eat."

She took a seat at the large wooden kitchen table. The garden was in darkness, but she could make out the reflection of water as it bounced off the tile of the terrace.

"It's beautiful. How old is this villa?" she asked.

"This villa was built in the mid-eighteen-hundreds to replace a crumbling home that my family had owned since the fifteen-hundreds. This land actually housed many crusaders during the Fourth Crusade." He brought her a cold glass of mineral water. "Drink it—the limes are actually mine too."

Shay took a sip. "Crusaders? How do you know?"

"Everybody knows," he said offhandedly. "Did you not learn about the Crusades in school?"

"No, it really wasn't on our curriculum."

Dante *tsked* under his breath. "The Lido was home to about ten thousand crusaders, spurred on by Pope Innocent III to sack Constantinople. They were blockaded here for a time because they could not afford to pay for the ships being built. In fact, some of my ancestors fought in the battle of Zara, but it wasn't until the fifteen-hundreds that my family gained notoriety and inherited the royal title. Of course, as this was my mother's family's home, my royal title has nothing to do with that at all. It's just a bit of interesting family history."

"I'm afraid I don't know much about my family at all."

Dante cocked an eyebrow. "Don't you?"

"No. Labadie is a French name. That much I know. My father's family came to New Orleans before it was purchased by the Americans. When it was still part of France, they, I believe, drifted down from the Maritimes in Canada during the Seven Years' War. Mostly Cajun."

"Seven Years' War?" Dante asked.

"Oh, didn't you learn about that in school?" Shay teased, and they both laughed at that.

"How does leftover risotto sound?" he asked. "Or perhaps some cheese?"

"Risotto sounds fine."

Dante went to heat the food and Shay glanced around the kitchen. She didn't do much cooking; she knew how to cook on cookstoves or an open fire. Basically anything that was propane-operated, because sometimes where she was working there might not always be electricity or even clean water.

This kitchen was opulent to her.

Even her mother's kitchen hadn't been this nice.

And then after Katrina, when the house had been condemned and her mother was dying from the effects of the mold she'd picked up in her lungs after the dikes had burst and flooded their home, the small run-down kitchen had been absolutely destroyed. Shay had had to go back into the home and try to salvage anything she could.

Only there had been nothing left to salvage, really.

A few pictures and birth certificates that had been stored in a flood-proof and fireproof box. And whatever else her mother had managed to cram into her carryall when she'd climbed out through the attic to the roof, waiting for help as the floodwaters rose.

"You look sad, *cara*."

"Do I?" she asked.

"Sì." He set the plate of risotto in front of her and then sat down next to her with his own plate. "Is something wrong?"

"No, I'm just tired." She plastered a fake smile on her face and took a bite of the risotto. "Oh, my goodness, this is so good."

He grinned. "I like to cook."

"You're not a traditional prince, then."

His brow furrowed. "What do you mean, 'traditional'?"

"You're a surgeon, you like to work with your hands and you cook. You don't have any servants."

He laughed. "I do have a lady come and clean my house, but you're right, I do most of it on my own. My maternal grandfather was a winemaker. He had a large vineyard in Tuscany and, though he was extremely wealthy, he taught me the value of hard work. I enjoy it."

"Well, you're good at it. I'm afraid my cooking would not be up to par. The only thing I can make, if I have the ingredients and the patience, is *boudin*."

"What is *boudin*?"

"A sausage stuffed with rice and green peppers."

"I would like to try that sometime."

Shay chuckled. "I'm not sure I'm up to *boudin* making at the moment."

"I can get you all the ingredients here."

"I'm sure you can, but I have a simulation course and training to run. Not to mention I'm to assist you in surgery. I'm here for work, Dante. Nothing else."

He frowned. "I'm passionate about my job too, but you have to live life as well. Work is not life."

"It is for me."

"And what happens when you have the child?" he asked. "Our child. Are you going to ignore our child for work?"

"No," she snapped. "I will balance it. A woman can work and be a mother. I think seeing me work will be a good example for our child."

Dante sighed. "I'm not saying that at all. Of course it's a good example, but you said you don't do anything *but* work. What do you do for fun?"

And the question caught her off guard, because really she didn't do much.

When she was on assignment, she put her whole heart and soul into the job.

There was no time for much else.

"You know what, I'm really tired. Is there a place I can sleep?"

"Of course, follow me."

Shay followed Dante out of the kitchen and up the winding staircase to the second floor. There were many rooms and a large open area with a couch and a desk. A living room. He led her to the back of the house and flicked on a light.

"This is the only room with a bed in it at the moment. When you move in, I'll move out of here."

"This is your room?"

"*Sì*, it is also the only bedroom with a private bathroom. I can use the one downstairs. It is no trouble."

"Where will you sleep?"

"The couch. I have some work to do. I'm not tired yet. You rest."

"I can't kick you out of your bedroom."

"You can." He smiled. "Get some rest and we'll talk about our plans for marriage tomorrow, but only if the results are positive."

"Sure. Okay." She rolled her eyes. Dante was so stubborn, so untrusting.

He nodded and shut her in his bedroom. Shay sighed and sat down on the edge of his large bed, sinking down into the soft duvet.

Tomorrow she'd tell him that it wasn't a good idea.

They weren't going to get married.

It was a foolish idea.

She lay down on the bed and thought about how she was going to tell him her reasons, but before she could get too far into her plans she drifted off into a deep, sound sleep.

CHAPTER FOUR

THE INCESSANT RINGING woke Shay up. And it took her a moment to realize where she was. She scrubbed a hand over her face and dug her phone out of her purse. It was Aubrey.

"Hello?" she said, trying not to sound too groggy.

"Are you okay?" Aubrey asked excitedly on the other end.

"Fine, just…you woke me up."

"Where did you sleep? I called last night and Danica told me that you were staying with Dr. Affini at his home and she's to send your belongings there."

"No. I'm not staying here permanently. I'll call Danica and tell her. It was just for last night. It's a long story." Shay sighed.

"Well, I told you to tell Dante about the baby, not to move in with him," Aubrey teased.

Shay laughed. "It's the pregnancy hormones that made me do it."

"I'll say."

"Where are you today?" Shay asked, hoping Aubrey was nearby. She needed to talk to her face-to-face. Aubrey had taken an assignment outside Venice but did move around a bit in Italy.

"Actually, I'm in Venice today, believe it or not."

"I'll tell you all about it at lunch, then. When is your lunch break?" Shay asked.

"Two. Do you want to meet for lunch at Braddicio's near the hospital? I heard it was good. And I know where that is."

"Sounds good," Shay said, trying to stifle a yawn. "I'll explain everything there."

"Okay, be careful."

Shay disconnected the call and then headed to the bathroom, where she quickly showered before re-dressing in yesterday's clothes.

The bathroom was white and modern like the kitchen, except for the deep, large claw tub with a shower hose placed on a rack in the middle of the room. There were long windows and the blinds were closed. There was a bit of sunlight peeking through the sides of the roman shades.

She pulled on the string and drew open the blinds, gasping when she noticed French doors that led out to a rooftop terrace. She unlatched the French doors and headed outside. From the terrace, the master suite faced the Adriatic. She could see the blue water and the sandy beaches that made the Lido di Venezia a favorite spot for tourists.

She closed her eyes and drank in the scent of fruit trees flowering in the spring, mixed with sand and surf. When she looked down, she could see the high stone walls that bordered Dante's garden. The fruit trees, the olive tree and the small pool that Dante was currently swimming laps in.

Naked.

Shay meant to look away, but couldn't. She couldn't help but watch him. His bronze form cutting through the turquoise water like a blade. It was mesmerizing. And she recalled very vividly what it was like to run her hands over that muscular body, to feel him pressed against her, his strong arms around her, holding her. His lips on her skin. Her blood heated. Drawn to him, she was so weak.

Don't look. Go downstairs and catch a ferry back to Venice. Back to the place you're staying, so you won't be tempted.

And she was so tempted by Dante.

She tore her gaze away and collected her purse and made her way downstairs.

When she got to the stairs, she could smell coffee. It was inviting and she desperately wanted a cup, but coffee was off-limits. She made her way to the kitchen, just as Dante came walking in through the open terrace doors. He had a towel wrapped around his waist, but she got an eyeful of his broad, muscular chest.

"You're awake," he said, his deep voice making her quake with a sudden need for him.

"Yes." She tried to avert her eyes from him, because she remembered all too well that body. The touch of it, the taste of it, the way he felt in her arms, his kisses burning a path of fire across her skin. "I hope your pool is heated."

"*Sì*, it is. How did you sleep?"

"Very well. Your bed is very comfortable and I feel bad for taking it. I have a perfectly good bed where I'm staying."

"You're going to be my wife and you're carrying my child. *This* is now your place," he said matter-of-factly.

"Dante, I'm not going to be—"

"You need to eat," he said, cutting her off,

which made her grind her teeth a bit. Was he this annoying in Oahu or were her hormones amplifying his annoying, arrogant habits?

"I'm trying to talk to you, Dante."

He was looking in the fridge. "How does some fresh fruit and yogurt sound?"

Great.

And her stomach growled in response.

Traitor.

"Dante, this is serious. More serious than fruit and yogurt."

He turned around then, one of those dark brows cocked. "Oh?"

"I'm not going to marry you, Dante. We can't get married."

"*Cara*, the only way I can protect you and the baby is by marrying you."

"What about the paternity test?"

"Dr. Tucci called," Dante said offhandedly. "The results came in. The child is mine."

Shay tried not to roll her eyes. "I know that, but that doesn't change the fact that I can't marry you."

"It's not permanent—the marriage, I mean. There will be rules. You will have your own room, your own space."

"You're going to give up your bed for a year?"

"I'll get another bed and I'll finish the other bedroom up on the second floor. It's not a problem. And then I'll start on the nursery."

"Dante, it's not as easy as this." She ran her hand through her hair to stop her from pulling it out.

"Why can't it be? This is a business arrangement to protect our child, and my child will have my name. A good name," he said as he scooped fresh berries into a bowl. "Now eat your breakfast and I'll shower and change before we head back to the hospital."

Dante was shutting down any further discussion to the matter and that was highly frustrating for Shay. She couldn't remember him being this stubborn before. He didn't even want to discuss the matter. Didn't he know what he was doing? He was going to blame her in a year for ruining his life.

Just as her father had done all the times when he'd been unhappy. Which had been a lot.

Sure, there had been moments when her father had been happy, but they had been few and far between. Now she couldn't even remember them.

She couldn't even remember her father's face.

All the pictures of him had been lost during Katrina, except for one that her mother had clutched to her chest when she'd taken her last breaths. And Shay had been so angry that her father had left them that way, left them in poverty, that she'd buried that picture with her mother in St. Louis Cemetery on Canal Street in New Orleans.

At least Dante wanted to give their child his name. Dante was offering their child roots, history. Permanence.

Something she couldn't give their child. Not really. He had land that was centuries old. Other than the house that Katrina had destroyed, there was no childhood home. Her mother and her always moving.

It still haunted her, the looks, the heartache of her mother, and she couldn't put her child through that. Even if it meant that she would be protected from the paparazzi. She didn't need that protection. She could take care of herself. She'd been in worse situations before and had managed.

You weren't pregnant before.

She shook that niggling thought from her head. She also couldn't help but wonder what Dante had to gain by marrying her, by supporting her.

She had a hard time believing it was just for the sake of the child.

Just marry him. Take the protection. Do your work and give your child access to his or her father.

The only thing that would be different in her situation was that she would never pine over a man who didn't want her. She wouldn't waste away as her mother had. She couldn't stay in Italy and rely on a man to help her raise her child, even if that man was her baby's father.

She was stronger than that.

He'd watched her sleep. He hadn't meant to go back into the room, but when he'd been on the couch last night she'd been all he could think about.

Shay had been plaguing his thoughts since their stolen night together in Oahu and now she was under his roof. Carrying his child.

And this morning, Dr. Tucci had confirmed what he'd known, deep down. He was just too afraid to hope, too afraid of being hurt to let himself believe it.

Shay had always been beautiful, but now, pregnant with his child, she was even more so and he couldn't help but think of the night of passion they'd had together. The night that had brought about this baby and their reunion.

The first woman he'd been with since Olivia and he'd had no qualms about taking her to his bed that night months ago. He'd dated since Olivia, but never had he made love to another woman until Shay. Usually he would talk himself out of it, but with Shay the desire had been too great.

He'd wanted her.

He *still* wanted her. That had never changed. He still desired her. The urge to take her in his arms and kiss her again was too much to bear.

She was in his villa. In his bed.

He'd sneaked into his bedroom, now her bedroom, to check on how she was doing. He hadn't been able to help himself.

Shay had been sleeping, but she'd been huddled in a ball in the middle of the bed, shivering. He had forgotten that he'd left a window open. Even though it was spring and temperatures were rising, the nights were still chilly. Especially the breeze coming off the Adriatic and the lagoon.

So he'd covered her with a blanket, made sure she was comfortable.

As in the taxi, he'd wanted to touch the rounded swell of her belly, but he wasn't sure.

Dante hadn't wanted her to wake, so he'd backed away and gone back to the living room, where he'd spent the night tossing and turning on the couch.

He wasn't sure what he was doing by asking her to marry him. He'd never intended to get married after what happened with Olivia, even if that meant he was going to lose everything. The vineyards, the villa and the inheritance.

The money didn't matter to him so much, but losing his grandfather's vineyard and this villa was what was crushing him. Now Shay was pregnant with his child and all his problems were solved.

Were they?

Why did he feel so guilty about this situation? And he couldn't help but think of his own parents' loveless marriage. Well, loveless on his father's part, because even though his father insisted that he'd loved their mother, a man who loved a woman wouldn't cheat on her repeatedly as their father had.

Perhaps the guilt stemmed from the fact that it seemed too easy that his problems were solved.

Shay had made it clear that she didn't want to marry him. She didn't love him.

He didn't want to ruin her life by forcing her to marry him, but it was the best thing for the baby.

He could protect them. He was going to be a father.

Why did it have to be her to come to Venice and not Daniel? Only, if she hadn't, would he ever have known about his child? He sometimes wondered if fate had a twisted sense of humor. Nonetheless, she was here and pregnant with his child and he was going to do right by them.

Both of them.

He was going to protect them from the paparazzi and anyone else who wanted a piece of the Affini name. He quickly had a shower in the main suite's bathroom, to wash the chlorine from his skin. He noticed that the French doors leading to the terrace were open and he wondered if Shay had ended up out there and seen him in the pool.

When he went for his morning swim, he didn't even think about putting on a bathing suit. He wasn't used to it, but if Shay was going to move in with him he'd have to remind himself of common decency.

Dante got dressed and ready to go back to the hospital for his shift in the emergency room. He had to complete rounds with students, check on his patients, including Mr. Sanders from yesterday.

When he came back downstairs, Shay was pacing, having finished her yogurt and berries. She shot him a look of frustration, but he didn't care. There was going to be no more talk about it. They were going to get married. He was going to take care of them.

By marrying her he could gain control over the vineyard and the villa, and then he could properly take care of them. His father wouldn't have any hand in it. His child's inheritance would be safe. He wouldn't sell off the estate, the land, piece by piece as his father was doing. His child would never look on him with disdain, the way he looked upon his father.

He would never hurt his child. He would be a better man than his father was.

And this was definitely his child, unlike what had happened with Olivia, when the child he'd thought was his hadn't been.

"You told me it was mine! I believed you."

She shrugged. "I wanted to marry you."

"Why? If the child wasn't mine..."

"The title. The name. Affini is respected."

"You were going to let me believe that your baby was mine, but really it's another man's? A man you were having an affair with before we even got together. Why?"

"Oh, come on, Dante. I don't love you. You don't love me. Not really. You were just excited about the prospect of family, of settling down and raising a child. I don't want that. I thought you were different. I thought we'd go to parties and hire a nanny."

"I never wanted that. That was how I was raised. I don't want that for my child."

She glared at him with those dark, hardened eyes. "Well, it's a good thing this child isn't yours."

"Are you ready to go?" he asked, shaking away that painful memory.

"I've been more than ready. I finished my breakfast a while ago. I would've left sooner, but I didn't know my way back to catch the water taxi. I'm a bit turned around here."

"We'll take the ferry to Venice—it's running

right now—or a *vaporetto* if we miss the ferry. Although the water buses are smaller than the ferry, I prefer the ferry, but they do the job."

He led her out the front door and locked up. It was a beautiful sunny day and everybody was out on the street. He put his arm through her arm.

"What're you doing?" she asked.

"Just leading you. Making sure you don't step out into the street."

"I've been all over the world in worse situations than this, in worse conditions than this. I'm not going to just step out into the street," she teased, the smile replacing the frown of worry that had been there moments ago.

"Nonetheless it is my pleasure to do so."

And it was. He liked walking with her. And he couldn't remember the last time he'd had company to work. It was nice.

They walked in silence down the Gran Viale Santa Maria Elisabetta toward the ferry landing. The ferry was there; they paid their fare and got on board just before it departed. He walked her up to the top deck to enjoy the sun and the breeze off the lagoon.

She was still slightly frustrated with him as she

leaned over the railing to look out over the water. He could tell by the way her brow was furrowed and her lips were pursed together.

"How was your breakfast? Was it adequate?" he asked.

"It was good," she said seriously. He chuckled, and then she smiled again. "It was good. Thank you."

"I'm glad to hear it. You have to remember to eat small meals all day long. It's the best for you and the baby."

"I know," she said.

"Do you have a doctor here in Venice yet?"

"No, I have to find one."

"I could send you to the clinic to talk to my brother. He's a family physician."

"Don't you think it would be odd that your brother would be my doctor in this situation?" she asked.

"Hmm, perhaps you're right. You need to go see Dr. Tucci, then. He's the ob-gyn that did the paternity test. He works in the hospital. He's quite good and he speaks English as well, as you know. He's one of the best."

"Dr. Tucci—that's good to know. I wasn't sure

who to go see. I wasn't sure that he worked in the hospital. I liked him."

"I would like to go to the appointment," Dante said.

"You want to go to my appointments?" Her finely arched eyebrows rose in surprise.

"Of course. It's my baby. I'm concerned about its health too."

"Yes, of course you would be." She sighed. "When we get to the hospital, I will make an appointment on my next break, but this morning I'm swamped. I have to plan the first simulation. The trainees are with another physician this morning, so that gives me time to plan an exercise they would face in the field."

Intrigued, he asked, "What were you thinking of?"

"I was thinking of a natural disaster, like a flood or forest fire."

He nodded. "That sounds good. You should do a flood. There're lots of floods here, especially when the big cruise ships come into the lagoon and they flood San Marco's *piazza* quite often. I mean, look what happened to Mr. Sanders in the *vaporetto* that was capsized because of one of those cruise ships and the big bow waves."

"I understand that. Flooding would be a big deal here, especially since this city is basically sitting on wooden planks. I'm sure that you face that issue all the time, but this is a city. These trainees will be going out into Third World countries where the flooding is different. Where the conditions are not so sanitary."

"Have you ever been in a flood where the conditions are not so sanitary?" he asked.

Shay frowned, her gaze drifting out over the water. "Yes, yes, I have."

"Where?"

"New Orleans," she said in a faraway voice. "Katrina."

She turned and looked away from him. It looked as if there were tears in her eyes as she said it.

"I'm sorry, *cara*," he apologized. "I didn't mean to bring up something that would be hard for you. I forgot...you're from New Orleans, aren't you?"

"Yes, it was terrible. The conditions were so bad."

"It wasn't just the hurricane, though?"

"No, it was after that. I was in school, training at the hospital and helping people escape. Taking care of those who couldn't flee. First we got out the infants, and then moved down the priority list. It was pretty scary. I was one of the last people to leave as the hospital flooded."

"I bet that was scary," he said, placing his hand over hers and giving it a reassuring squeeze. There wasn't much more he could say. He'd read about the devastation.

"That was the first and worst flood I've ever been in. I've been in other floods, but Katrina was definitely the worst," she said quietly, looking off into the distance. "I don't really want to talk about it, if you don't mind."

He nodded. "I'm sorry for bringing it up, *cara*. I didn't mean to cause you pain."

"It's okay. You didn't hurt me. You're right, they could have to deal with flooding in a city like this, a city like New Orleans, during a natural disaster. They could be posted anywhere. The conditions weren't sanitary in New Orleans. There was no power, no clean water. So yeah, maybe I'll do the first simulation in a setting like this. A setting where everything you thought you had, because you're not in a Third World country and are used to having, is no longer available. You have to learn to boil water in unsanitary conditions, where your supplies can run out. Thanks for that, Dante. I think that's what I'll do today."

"I'm always here to help. I'm part of this program too. I wish I could help you more, but I have rounds in the emergency room today. And I would like to check on Mr. Sanders."

"Did you hear anything about his condition after Dr. Prescarrie saw him?" she asked.

Dante sighed. "Yes, there was some damage to his spinal cord—it's bruised and there's swelling. We're hoping his paralysis isn't permanent. He's in the ICU. The internal bleeding has stopped. That's the main thing."

"That's good," she said. "I hope his paralysis isn't permanent. That's the last thing he needs on a trip of a lifetime, all because a cruise ship taking it too fast caused a *vaporetto* to capsize."

He nodded. "Yes, it's these things that annoy us Venetians about the tourist industry. So many tourists."

"You don't like tourists?"

"We like them. I mean, it's a way of life, but then there're things like the cruise ships coming in too fast and flooding San Marco's *piazza*, and there are issues with overcrowding. It's not the same as it was when I was young."

"I bet it's not," she said. "New Orleans gets tourists, especially during Mardi Gras. It's insane around the French Quarter. You can't walk around anywhere. It's just packed full of people."

"So you understand what I'm talking about."

"I do get it," she said. "They bleach Bourbon Street every night."

"Bleach the street?"

"Oh, yes." She grinned. "Bourbon Street is a very popular party street. There are a lot of bars and people drink a lot and sometimes they can't always find a bathroom."

He wrinkled his nose. "That's terrible."

"It is," she said. "Every night after last call and into the early morning the street cleaners go out and bleach the street with lemon and bleach. It's very citrusy if you walk down Bourbon Street just after they've sprayed it, but if you walk ahead of the cleaners, like I did one night trying to get to work, you learn to appreciate the bleach."

They laughed together at that as the ferry pulled into the docks.

It was a short walk from the ferry to the hospital. And there wasn't any press around. Dante made sure she got to her office and was settled, before he headed to his.

"Shay, if you need anything, please have me paged. I'm here for you, *cara*."

She nodded. "Thank you, but I've arranged to meet my friend today for lunch and talk to her about a few things, because I'm honestly not sure about this, Dante. I mean, a marriage of convenience… I can't agree to that."

He held up his hand, cutting her off. "It's for the best. Trust me."

"How can I trust you? We barely know each other."

He understood that. He understood about not trusting someone. His trust had been shattered when Olivia broke his heart.

"You just have to," he said, and he walked away.

Not even sure that he could trust her either.

Dante made his rounds pretty quickly, which always gave him a bad feeling because when the emergency room was quiet it would inevitably become busy in the near future. Which meant trauma.

After he did his rounds and checked on the stability of Mr. Sanders, who was doing well in the intensive care unit, he headed back to his office. He resisted the urge to go and find Shay to see how she was coming along with the simulation planning because he wanted to give her some space. He had a feeling that he was overwhelming her and he didn't blame her one bit. He was feeling a bit overwhelmed himself.

When he walked into his office, he saw Enzo standing in front of his desk, his back to him. The expensive suits his brother always wore gave him away.

"Enzo, aren't you supposed to be at the clinic?"

Enzo turned around and flashed him that impish smile he'd had since he was a young boy. "Is that any way to talk to your brother? Not even a *ciao* and asking how I am doing, just straight to the point of why I'm here?"

"Yes, usually it is. You're a pain in my side." Dante laughed.

Enzo just shook his head. "I have some good news—"

"Did you do what I asked?" Dante said, interrupting him.

"Yes, I left a message with someone from the United World Wide Health Association who was at the house. I told her where Shay was and where she was going to be moving to. She said she would try to find time to pack Shay's personal belongings, but I don't know."

"Well, they haven't yet," Dante said.

Enzo shrugged. "I can't help that. I did what you asked me to. I wasn't about to go into some woman's room and rummage through her things. Especially if she's rooming with another woman. I really don't feel like being beaten up by a bunch of United World Wide Health Association workers. I have a practice to run and I'm going to be getting one of those United World Wide Health Association nurses in my clinic soon to deal with the tourists."

"You don't sound very happy about that," Dante said.

Enzo shrugged again. "Am I ever happy about stuff like that? It is what it is. Maybe she'll have a lighter hand with the tourists. Sometimes I don't have enough patience with them."

"So intolerant," Dante teased.

"Look, I have some news. Do you want to hear it or not?"

"*Sì*, I want to hear it."

"I have a friend who works for the civil court. I explained your situation and they are very aware of our situation with respect to our inheritance and the trust fund."

"Oh, yes?" Dante was now very interested.

"And instead of the four-day waiting period to get your Nulla Osta they were able to give it to me today. All you have to do is get Shay to sign it stating that there is no impediment for you two to marry, and you can marry today, provided you have two witnesses."

"I hope you'll be one of the witnesses."

"I'll try. Truly," Enzo said. "I want to make sure this is seen through. I'm still worried, Dante. I still have my misgivings about this."

"I know you do, but, trust me, Shay is pregnant with my child. The paternity result said so. I met her at that conference in Hawaii months ago. We had one night of passion. We did use protection, but you know that doesn't always work. And now she's expecting my child."

Enzo nodded. "Don't you think it's funny, though, that she came here? I mean, people know about us. The paparazzi follow us around even though we have restraining orders. Everyone knows our father is a womanizer and has sold off pieces of Affini land, just so he could pay for all his mistresses, and that he'll eventually sell off our mother's land too if he gets the chance. Affini men are cheaters, both in matters of money and women. It was the same with his father too. Affini men are a bunch of womanizers. What if she hears about that?"

"What if she does?" Dante asked, getting impatient. He knew all this. Why was Enzo so worried?

"Isn't that why Olivia went after you? She could claim that you were not being faithful to her, even though she was ultimately not faithful to you. Women like that are just looking for a handout."

"I am aware of the situation, Enzo. Because it's happened to me. It won't happen this time. This is my child. With Olivia it was different. She was pregnant before we met—that's how I knew the child wasn't mine. It was better I found out. It hurt a lot at the time, that's true, but Shay *is* pregnant with my child. I'm going to take care of them even if I have to give them a handout. I'm going to support her. I'm going to make sure my child is taken care of. That's the kind of person that I am."

Enzo shook his head. "This is why I don't want to get involved with any woman. Just give me casual relationships."

"Casual can lead to a baby too," Dante said. "Look what happened here. Shay and I were only ever going to be a onetime thing and now she's pregnant with my child. If it wasn't for the fact that I was approaching my thirty-fifth birthday, I wouldn't be pushing this marriage so hard. I would support the child, don't get me wrong," Dante said quickly. "Because, unlike you, I want to be a father."

There had been so many times when he was in that villa that he'd felt lonely. He wouldn't admit it, but it was true. It hurt thinking about what could've been with Olivia if she hadn't betrayed his trust, if that child had been his. He wanted a family. Despite the fact that his father was a womanizer who had broken his mother's heart. He wanted what he'd never had as a child. A happy family.

Love from both parents.

What his mother had mourned, because she'd had that as a child and hadn't been able to give it to her sons.

Dante had loved his mother. She was a good mother. He loved Enzo and having a brother. He'd loved spending time with his maternal grandparents in Tuscany. Every summer they would spend their time there when they weren't in school. Then there were the times his mother would take them to the dilapidated villa that was now his home. They would spend time running on the sandy beaches at the Lido, eating olives and picking fresh fruit.

It was a happy time.

On the Lido they had been away from the hustle and bustle. From the lonely nights when their parents had gone to parties and entertained. From the fights and arguments their parents had had. From the heartbreaking cries of their mother as her heart had broken more every time their father had cheated.

He wasn't going to do that. Enzo was more afraid of becoming a womanizer than Dante was, but Olivia had crushed every little piece of trust he'd had and he wasn't sure he ever wanted to take the risk of having what he'd always wanted.

Family.

Shay showing up in Venice pregnant was scary. He was terrified, but he was going to do the right thing. Even if the marriage was for show and nothing was going to come of things between the two of them, he was going to have a child. An heir. He was going to be a part of that child's life forever. He didn't take his duty lightly.

He was going to make sure his child was happy. His child wasn't going to suffer the way he and Enzo had suffered. He wasn't going to hurt Shay, or his child.

"Come on, let's go get Shay to sign this." Dante took the forms from Enzo. "Then you can meet her and see for yourself that she's nothing like Olivia."

"I look forward to meeting her. Another time, though. I have work to take care of."

"You can come meet her here before you go."

They walked through the halls of the hospital to the other side where the simulation training was going to take place, but they found that Shay's office was locked. Dante knocked, but there was no answer.

A nurse walked by.

"She went out for lunch," the nurse said.

"Do you know where?" Dante asked.

"*Sì*, Braddicio's, which isn't far."

"Do you know when she'll be back?" Dante asked.

"I don't know," the nurse said. "The simulation is ready, but the trainees are still working with

Dr. Carlo, so it's been postponed until they are done working with Dr. Carlo."

Dante cursed under his breath. *"Grazie."*

"Well, now what?" Enzo asked. "I don't have much longer before I have to get back to the clinic."

"How about we go to the restaurant? I need to talk to her privately away from here anyway. You can distract the girlfriend she's having lunch with while I talk to Shay."

"No good," said Enzo. "I'm truly sorry, but you're on your own."

Dante cursed under his breath. "You're a thorn in my side, Enzo."

And all Enzo did was grin.

CHAPTER FIVE

SHAY WALKED INTO BRADDICIO'S, which was tucked down a small canal, off the main canal near the hospital. She'd been here before. It was a nice Italian bistro, dark and romantic, and the food was good. Shay loved it here. When she went inside, Aubrey was already sitting there, waiting. She looked worried as she watched the door.

Shay headed to the booth in the corner where Aubrey was waiting for her. When Aubrey's gaze landed on her, she could see the relief wash over her face.

"Oh, thank goodness," Aubrey said. "I've been so worried about you. You didn't go into too many details on the phone this morning and I figured you couldn't speak freely. I hopped a train for you, I'll have you know."

"I was fine, Aubrey. I was with Dante—the father of my child *and* a highly respected surgeon," she teased. "I was in very good hands."

"I know, I know. I was just concerned when you weren't at the house when I called last night. I know I pushed you to take this job here and to tell Dante about his child, but I didn't expect you to run off with him."

"I didn't."

"Clearly. Still, I was picturing all these horrible things happening to you." Aubrey grinned. "I'm relieved."

"What kind of horrible things? The worst he could do is lock me up in his villa…"

"He owns a villa?" Aubrey asked with surprise. "Where?"

"The Lido di Venezia."

"He has a villa on the Lido?" Aubrey asked, impressed. "Wow, Venice is expensive."

"He's a prince."

Aubrey's mouth dropped open, her eyes wide, and she shook her head. "A what?"

"A prince. The father of my baby is a prince. Yesterday when I tried to leave the hospital after my shift ended I was accosted by the paparazzi because my baby is the Affini heir." She'd lowered her voice, not that there were many people in the restaurant while they were having their lunch break, but, still, she didn't want someone to hear.

"So that's why he wants to marry you? Because he's a prince?"

"Something like that," Shay said. "He said he could protect me. He has a restraining order against the press. Once he had me in his arms, they didn't come back again. They didn't follow us to the Lido to bother us either."

Aubrey frowned. "He wants to marry you to *protect* you? That sounds a little old-fashioned. What did you say?"

"I told him no, of course, but he's so insistent. Which is why I wanted to talk to you."

"Do you *want* to marry him? I thought you didn't want to get married."

"I don't, but he wants to give his child his name. And it would be more of a business arrangement. Dante said it need only last a year."

"You don't need to be married for him to give your child his name, you know," Aubrey said.

"I know, right? I mean, it's just that he's royalty and their name is well-known—it's a legitimizing thing apparently. And…with my work… well, I could continue to do my work if he was involved."

"You don't have to be married for him to be involved in your child's life. Or for you to be able to continue with your career, Shay."

"I know. I'm so confused. When I woke up in his bed this morning in his villa, it felt right being with him, but… I don't know."

Aubrey's eyes widened. "You spent the night in his bed, in his villa?"

"Yes." Shay winced as Aubrey groaned. "But he was the perfect gentleman and slept downstairs on the sofa all night," she added quickly.

"Oh, Shay, are you still attracted to him?"

"Yes."

Aubrey looked even more concerned then. "And he only wants to be married for a year? That seems weird."

"I know." Shay sighed. "It sounds a little too good to be true, but there you have it. I don't know what to do."

"Well, at least he wants to be involved with his child's life."

"Yes, that much he does," Shay agreed.

"That's a good thing." Aubrey had issues with her own father, just as Shay did. Which was probably why they'd bonded so quickly when they'd met in their first years during the UWWHA. Aubrey was the one who had been so insistent that

Shay find Dante and tell him about the baby. Aubrey was also the one who'd found out about this job and suggested that Shay take it when Daniel dropped out.

Shay didn't know what to do, which was why she was glad Aubrey was visiting today. She needed to talk it out. That was how she rationalized things.

"I wonder what's in it for him," Aubrey mused.

"That's exactly what I was thinking. I don't understand. Couldn't someone just offer to get the mother of their child on their restraining order without them having to marry?"

"Yeah," Aubrey said. "I'm not familiar with how that works here. I'm not too familiar with Italian laws."

"I don't know what to do," Shay said. "He promises that the marriage won't interfere with my work and that it's on paper only. Once the year is up, I'm free to go. He'll grant me a painless divorce. No fighting over custody, which we'll share. We're going to have contracts drawn up and everything."

"It just sounds *off*, Shay." Aubrey didn't look convinced. "Please promise me that you'll get a lawyer to look over everything. Especially when dealing with Italian laws as a foreigner."

"I know. I will. I just want my child to have their father in their life."

Aubrey nodded sadly. "I understand that. I get that, but you have to protect yourself too."

"There is nothing to protect myself from. I don't own any assets. It's Dante who should be worried, even though I have no interest in his money. Or his land. Or his title."

Or him? a little voice in her head asked. She shook that thought away. She did have an interest in him. A big interest, which was what had got her into this situation in the first place. Only she would never hang on to past relationships. Once it was over, it was over. With Dante, it wasn't. There was something different about him.

You're carrying his baby, that's why.

She hadn't known she was pregnant for weeks after conception, yet she'd thought of Dante every day since they'd parted. So what was it about him? Why was Dante different from her other few fleeting relationships?

You've never been this attracted to someone before.

And she *was* attracted to Dante. She still desired him. Just being around him made her pulse quicken, her blood heat, and the urge to kiss him again was strong.

"I'm not just talking legal stuff."

"Oh?"

"You're attracted to him and yet you're agreeing to this cold and loveless marriage."

Blood rushed to Shay's cheeks and she groaned. "Yes."

"Tread carefully. I don't want you to get hurt."

"Why don't we order something? I'm starving," Shay said, keen to shake away thoughts of Dante and kissing him. "I haven't had anything to eat since this morning when he made me fresh fruit and yogurt."

Aubrey chuckled. "He made you fresh fruit and yogurt?"

"He's a good cook. I tasted the risotto he made the night before. It was delicious. He says he likes to do it."

"Well, that's at least something, because you are a terrible cook."

They both laughed at that as the waiter came over to take their order. Shay ordered a glass of Italian soda, while Aubrey got to have wine.

They continued talking about their work and

how Aubrey's work was going farther south in the country, and Shay talked about the simulations she was going to run the new trainees through. It was nice to chat like normal again. To not talk about babies or marriage.

"Oh, my," Aubrey said, perking up.

"What?"

Aubrey nodded at the door. "I think your husband-to-be just walked in."

Shay turned and saw Dante standing in the doorway of the restaurant.

"What is he doing here?"

Dante caught her gaze and then headed over to their table. By the firm set of his jaw and his tight gait he was on a mission.

"*Scusami*, I'm so sorry for intruding on your lunch." Dante smiled briefly, but charmingly, at Aubrey.

"What're you doing here, Dante?" Shay asked.

"I need to speak with you alone, Shay." Then he turned to Aubrey. "If you'll excuse us? This is important."

Aubrey was going to say something, because she didn't look too thrilled at having their lunch interrupted, but Dante turned his back on her. Shay sighed—this arrogant side was not what she was used to from Dante—and slid out of the booth. Dante led her away and Aubrey looked none too happy about being left alone. Her lips were thinned and her arms tightly folded across her chest.

Not a good sign. Dante didn't know what kind of trouble he was in.

"What, can't it wait until I go back to the hospital?" she asked.

"This." He held out a paper. "This is a Nulla Osta. If you sign it, we can get married this afternoon."

"Dante! This afternoon? We have to finish our shift and I haven't even agreed to marry you yet!" She rubbed her temple. "You're very persistent."

He grinned. "I know."

"Maybe I should get a lawyer."

"Shay, I promise you, you don't need a lawyer. This is just a form that states that there's nothing to stop us from getting married. You sign it and we head to the courthouse to get married now. I will provide you a contract outlining the details of our marriage within five days to a lawyer of your choosing."

"So, I have to stay married to you for a year?"

"*Sì.*"

"This is not a real marriage, though?" And warmth flooded in her cheeks as she asked that question. It was a polite way of saying that there would be no sex between them.

"Correct. You will have your own space at my villa."

"What happens after the year is up? You said I wouldn't have to fight for custody."

"*Sì*, we will have joint custody. I will take our child when you need to work. Our child will have my name and will be taken care of. You, as our child's mother, will be as well. Finally, our child will have dual citizenship."

"I don't know..." Then she thought of the schooling her child could receive with Dante's money and connections. The opportunities she'd never had as a bright child growing up in the lower ninth ward of New Orleans, moving around constantly. No roots. No family ties. No father.

She bit her lip.

Do it for your child.

"Where do I sign?" Shay asked.

Dante pulled out a pen, but before she could sign on the dotted line his pager went off. He pulled it out. "Incoming trauma. I knew it was too quiet this morning."

"We should go, then," Shay said.

"*Sì.*"

Shay turned and saw that Aubrey was frowning, her eyes narrowed as she glared at Dante.

"I have to go, Aubrey. There's incoming trauma," Shay said.

Aubrey nodded. "Don't worry. Go. I'll settle up and we'll talk later. I have a train to catch." It was as if Aubrey knew that Shay would agree to the marriage of convenience in the end.

Shay smiled and mouthed, "Thank you," as she left the restaurant with Dante. Her mind was still reeling with the fact she'd decided to marry him.

Even though she was terrified at the prospect.

Dante hated fires.

He hated when people were burned. He never did like it when people were injured, but burn victims always hit a little too close to home. His best friend had been caught in a fire and had received burns to seventy percent of his body. He'd lived for a few short days in complete agony.

And this situation was no different.

The young man was in pain and Shay was moving quickly in the chaos of a busy trauma room. He appreciated it. She knew what to do. He didn't have to tell her what to do. She just did it. She set up the IV with antibiotics and painkillers while Dante examined the extent of the burns.

"Was it a house fire?" Dante asked the paramedic who brought the patient in.

"*Sì*, it was."

Once Dante learned that, he changed his tactic. He knew that when some of the old houses caught fire, they were very enclosed and it wasn't just the burns that could kill.

It was the carbon monoxide poisoning in the blood. The patient's lungs could be scorched.

He could suffocate.

Dante immediately listened to the patient's chest. His breath was hoarse, labored. He tilted the patient's head back and examined his throat, to see black.

"We need to intubate him," Dante said to Shay. "Get me an intubation kit."

She nodded and went over to the cabinets in the bay, pulling out an intubation kit. Dante tilted the patient's head back once more and quickly intubated him. Shay bagged him once the tube was in, pumping air into the man's lungs until they could get him up into the ICU.

There wasn't much he could do for the third-degree burns in the trauma bay.

The man's blood pressure was high and he was now intubated. They had to get him stable, and then they could take him into surgery where they would clean his burns and help prevent infection.

"I want a CBC drawn. I need to see how much carboxyhemoglobin is in his blood."

Shay nodded. "I'll do that."

"When he's stable and we have his labs back, we'll get him into the operating room."

Dante watched as Shay hooked the man up to the ventilator. The man was now in an induced coma, but it was good. This way he wasn't in pain.

Once they had the patient as stable as they could, porters came to take the patient up to the ICU. Dante and Shay removed their gloves and moved to the next bay, making their rounds through the influx of patients that had come through, but there was no one that needed immediate attention, as the burn victim had needed.

"I'd better get to my simulation training," Shay said. "I just got a page that they're ready for me now that Dr. Carlo is done with them."

"Do you need any help with that?" Dante asked.

"No, but maybe you could walk me out of the emergency room to my office? I still haven't got the lay of the land yet."

He chuckled. "Of course."

Dante led the way out of the emergency room.

"How long will the training last?" Dante asked.

"Why?"

"The courthouse closes at five."

"Oh. Right. Do we have to do it today? I signed the form. Can't we wait? I promised I would marry you. I won't run. I can't."

She was nervous and Dante found it endearing.

"*Sì*, we have to do it today because you signed the form and dated it."

"Okay, I'll make sure I'm done in time. How long will it take and who will be our witnesses?"

"It should only take a few minutes and I've asked Enzo, but he might be busy. Do you think your friend Aubrey will step in?"

"No, she's headed back to Rome, where she's working at the moment. And my roommate is packing my belongings, since I'm apparently moving in with you tonight."

"That makes me very happy." Dante grinned that charming lopsided, dimpled smile that made her weak at the knees.

And it was true. Once she was under his roof, then he would be more at ease about this whole situation. There he could take care of her and take care of their baby.

"Does it make you happy?" she asked.

"It does. This will benefit us both, Shay."

"That's what I can't figure out. How does this benefit you?"

"By having the baby in my life, that's how it benefits me. Being a father is an honor and something I have always wanted. My name, and passing it down, is important to me." He didn't know why he couldn't tell her the real reason, why he didn't tell her about the trust fund, other than the fact that the last time he'd told someone about it, she had used him. Shay knew he was a prince, knew that he owned the villa, but she really didn't understand the scope of what was at stake.

And he just didn't trust her enough yet to tell her.

He couldn't tell her.

"So, when should I come back?" Dante asked as they stood in front of the training room.

"Two hours should suffice. The simulation is ready to go and they have to complete it in a certain time or else they don't pass."

"You're tough," Dante teased.

She grinned. "Working with the United World Wide Health Association isn't an easy ticket. It's hard work. I was put through my paces and I plan to do the same for them."

"I don't doubt it. I'll come back in two hours, then, and we'll make it official. That way you can move freely throughout Venice. The restraining order will protect you and our baby."

Shay nodded and headed into the training room.

Dante turned and walked back to the emergency room, but first he pulled out his phone and tried to call Enzo. There was no answer and it went straight to voice mail.

"Can you meet Shay and I at the city hall at half past four? She signed the papers and we're going to make it official." He disconnected the call.

His stomach twisted at the thought of Shay becoming his wife.

Having a wife was the last thing he'd wanted, but also something he'd secretly always longed for.

He was so close to having it all, but then a sense of dread sank in his stomach and he couldn't help but wonder when it would all end.

When he would lose it all.

He'd learned very young that he couldn't take life for granted. That happiness was fleeting. So when would all of this be snatched away from him?

He hated the fact he was such a pessimist. He was a surgeon. He was supposed to be an optimist.

Only he didn't feel so optimistic at the moment.

He was only feeling dread over what the future held.

CHAPTER SIX

SHAY COULDN'T FOLLOW most of the civil ceremony, but she understood when the judge pronounced them man and wife.

"You may kiss your bride," the officiant said in English.

Shay's pulse raced. She hadn't anticipated that a kiss would be part of this marriage.

Since she'd agreed to the marriage she kept trying to think of it as a business arrangement for the benefit of their child, but now as she held Dante's hand, staring up into his dark brown eyes as his wife, the prospect of kissing him made her insides quiver. Her body responded with the familiar ache, because it knew what his kisses were like.

How they enflamed her.

Dante bent down and pressed his lips against hers briefly, but in that moment a jolt of electricity raced through her, her body recalling every kiss he'd shared with her. It lit a fire in her that had never been extinguished. This marriage of convenience was going to be hard.

Dante stepped away quickly, pulling at his collar again as the officiant led them to where they were to sign the certificate.

The court had standby witnesses, who signed their names after Shay and Dante had finished signing theirs.

She accepted congratulations graciously, but there was a little voice in the back of her head reminding her that this marriage was a sham.

That she shouldn't be here.

This wasn't real.

And it really wasn't.

She'd just entered into a marriage of convenience with the father of her baby.

This is for the baby. Dante won't leave the baby. He wants to be a father. He's not like your father.

As they stepped outside she took a deep breath to calm her erratic pulse.

"Shall we celebrate?" Dante asked as they left the courthouse.

"I'd rather have a nap," Shay teased. "I do need to collect my things if I'm moving in with you. And your lawyer will need to start looking into extending my visa."

"*Sì*, he will, and as for collecting your things— we can do that." Dante walked to the edge of the Grand Canal and flagged down a gondola.

"What're you doing?" Shay asked, bewildered.

"Flagging down a gondola. That's how we'll get to your residence. Or rather your former residence."

"A water taxi will do."

"I like this way better." He winked at her, those dark eyes of his twinkling, sending her pulse skittering.

Damn him.

"How do you know how to get to the United World Wide Health Association house?"

"Because it was my childhood home," Dante said quickly as a gondola pulled up. "Come on."

His childhood home?

He took her hand and helped her down the steps into the gondola.

"You know, we could've walked too. I don't think I've ever used the canal entrance before."

Dante smiled. "I know, but this is a celebration. We're married and the world is watching. We have to pretend that we're a happy couple out in public. You have just snagged one of Italy's most eligible bachelors."

Shay smiled ruefully as he took a seat beside her on the cushioned bench.

The gondolier used his long pole to push away from the canal ledge out into the Grand Canal. She hadn't done this before. Mostly she just walked where she needed to go. The United World Wide Health Association residence wasn't far from the hospital and Shay liked to walk, but as they slowly glided down the main canal she found herself relaxing into the ride. She could see smaller canals leading off the Grand Canal, overshadowed by old buildings and smaller bridges that connected one side to the other.

On the Grand Canal there were larger bridges, with tourists passing over them as the gondola glided underneath. She understood now why so many people loved this. Why it was popular with tourists. It was beautiful. It was calming and she was suddenly very aware that she was alone on a romantic gondola ride with Dante.

And he was so close, she could smell his masculine aftershave, feel his strong arm around her. His hand on her shoulder, his fingers making circles through the fabric of her scrubs, making her body yearn for something more.

You can't have any more. And Aubrey's warning about treading carefully went through her mind.

"So, the United World Wide Health Association residence was your childhood home?" she asked, trying to defuse the tension she was feeling and chasing the thoughts of kissing Dante away to something a little more tedious.

"*Sì*, my father sold it off a few years ago. He and my mother moved elsewhere." There was a hint of bitterness in Dante's voice.

"You sound sad about it."

"Annoyed," Dante said, and he ran his hand through his hair as he always seemed to do when he was distracted. "I didn't have as much of an attachment to that home as my younger brother did. I prefer the villa where I live and the vineyard in Tuscany."

"I would love to see the vineyard."

"You told me once that you never sightsee when you're on assignment. There is so much more to Italy than just Venice."

"Isn't that blasphemy?" she teased. "You're Venetian."

He smiled. "Perhaps, but I am Italian first."

The gondolier pulled up in front of the United

World Wide Health Association house, tying up his gondola as Dante asked him to wait. Dante climbed out and helped her out of the gondola.

"Why are you asking the gondolier to wait?" Shay asked. "I didn't think they crossed the lagoon."

"No, they don't, but I thought it would be nice to take the gondola down the Grand Canal back to the hospital before we make our way to the ferry docks."

Shay didn't respond as they walked into the rental house that had once been Dante's childhood home. The moment they stepped over the threshold his demeanor changed. She could tell by the way his body stiffened. He jammed his hands in his pockets and kept looking straight ahead.

Even though he'd said that he wasn't attached to this home, it clearly brought up some painful memories for him. She knew the look, because that was the way she'd felt the day she'd walked back into her mother's house after the floodwaters had receded. After FEMA had told her it was marked condemned and that she was allowed one last look inside before it was demolished.

Yet it still stood. They hadn't demolished it yet.

It was boarded up and covered with graffiti, sitting among the wrecks and ruin of the lower ninth ward homes. People toured the area now, which ticked Shay off no end.

It was macabre.

Don't think about it now.

"I'll just go collect my suitcase. I won't be too long."

He nodded and stood by the door. She went upstairs to her room.

She collected her few belongings and left. She was sad that she wasn't going to be living here. She'd always lived on-site wherever the United World Wide Health Association housed her.

This was a first, living off-site.

It was nerve-racking.

This is for your baby. It's only temporary. Just a year. You were going to take a year maternity leave anyways after this twelve-week assignment.

Still, a pang of homesickness washed over her.

She couldn't remember the last time she'd ever felt homesick and she wasn't sure if she ever did feel homesick.

This isn't your home.

Shay didn't have a home. And she never had, really. She and her mother were always moving and this was no different. Only it was. Dante was offering her permanence for a year and permanence for a lifetime for their child.

With a sigh she walked back downstairs. Dante met her halfway up the steps and took her suitcase from her.

"Is this it?" he asked.

She nodded. "Yes. Everything I own fits into that suitcase and my purse."

He gave her a strange look. "Strange."

"It's not strange. I travel a lot."

"Don't you have a home in New Orleans?"

"I have a place to stay, but it's not much." It was just a bed, a couple pieces of furniture. That was all. It was just a place to stay while she waited for assignments.

"Good thing you're moving in with me, then," Dante said as they went outside and he handed her suitcase to the gondolier.

"Why is that?" she asked.

"Because every child needs a place to call home."

Shay's stomach twisted in a knot and she resisted the urge to say something further. About how not every child was that lucky, but it wasn't about that. He was absolutely right. Every child deserved a home and by agreeing to marry Dante, even if on paper only, she was giving her child something she'd never had.

A home.

Which was why she'd agreed to this marriage of convenience in the first place.

And that was the most important thing.

Dante stood at the nurses' station in the emergency department filling out a newly discharged patient's chart. Soon Dr. Salzar would come and relieve him for the night shift. Dante wanted to make sure that everything was in order for the sign-off.

He glanced up to see Shay leading a group of United World Wide Health Association trainees through the emergency room. He smiled watching her. She'd been so busy since they'd got married, he rarely saw her.

It had been well over two weeks of just moving past each other like ships in the night. No more than a greeting and the odd quick meal. And then the last five mornings when he'd finished his swim she had already left, taking the first ferry across the lagoon. At night when he got home from his shift she was always fast asleep.

She wasn't totally at fault. He'd been busy preparing the contract for their marriage, and when the baby was born Dante's inheritance left by his mother in trust would be his at last. At least now with the marriage his father couldn't get his hands on it.

Almost three weeks now without really talking to Shay made him realize that he missed her.

What did you expect it to be like? It's not a real marriage. You're basically roommates.

Still, he wanted to get to know the mother of his child. This marriage might be keeping her here for the sake of their baby, but he found that he liked spending time with her when he saw her. And on the occasions when they worked together with the trainees he enjoyed his time with her and he found himself wanting more.

You can't have more. She's made it clear she doesn't want more.

Besides, the press were noticing the distance between them. He'd seen the headlines. He would have to talk to Shay later about putting on a better show of marriage. At least for the year. The last thing he needed was some kind of ridiculous headline to the effect that he was buying a baby or something.

"Dr. Affini?"

Dante turned around and his intern was standing behind him.

"How can I help you, Dr. Martone?"

"I have a patient in a trauma bay. I think you need to check his EKG."

Dante took the electronic chart from Dr. Martone and frowned when he saw the chart. The patient was a sixty-five-year-old man who'd presented with dizziness, nausea, shortness of breath and severe heartburn. The ST segment of the EKG was elevated.

"What do you think?" Dante asked as he flipped through the tests. Dante had his suspicions, but he was teaching Dr. Martone, who was fresh out of medical school and a quick learner.

"STEMI."

"Which stands for?"

"Segment elevation myocardial infarction," Dr. Martone answered.

"Let's go see the patient."

Dante followed his intern into the larger trauma bay. When he walked into the room, he saw the patient already had oxygen and that an IV was started. Shay walked into the bay on the other end of the open room.

"Do you need a hand, Dr. Affini?" she asked as she came up beside him.

"I do." He handed her the chart and went up to the patient. "*Buongiorno*, I'm Dr. Affini and I'll be taking care of you."

"It's a pleasure to meet you," the patient said, his breathing labored. "I'm Giovanni Scalzo."

"Can you tell me what brought you in here tonight, Mr. Scalzo?" Dante asked as he listened to the patient's chest.

"Indigestion," Giovanni said. 'I don't know what the fuss is all about. I was hoping for a prescription antacid."

Shay handed Giovanni an aspirin. "Mr. Scalzo, can you take this, please?"

Giovanni grinned up at Shay and Dante couldn't blame him.

"Anything for you, *cara*." Giovanni grinned again and took the aspirin.

Dante chuckled. "Do you have a cardiologist, Mr. Scalzo?"

Giovanni looked confused. "No."

Shay and he exchanged looks.

"Mr. Scalzo, I'm going to page our cardiologist on duty, Dr. Fucci, to come and take a look at your labs."

"Is something wrong with my heart?" Giovanni's monitors beeped as his blood pressure rose from panic.

Shay stepped forward and placed a hand on the patient's shoulder, instantly calming the patient down with the simple reassurance of touch.

"Don't worry, Mr. Scalzo, you're in good hands here. Your EKG was a little elevated and I'd like to run it by a specialist if that's okay with you?" Dante's question also calmed down Giovanni.

"*Sì*, that's good." Mr. Scalzo lay back against the bed. Dante watched his breathing become more labored.

"Are you in pain, Mr. Scalzo?" Shay asked.

"*Sì*, the heartburn burns my throat and my arms feel heavy."

"Give him some morphine," Dante said. Then he turned to his intern. "Page Dr. Fucci and prep the cath lab for a percutaneous coronary intervention."

"*Sì*, Dr. Affini," Dr. Martone said, taking back the chart.

Dante left the trauma bay. The next ninety minutes would be crucial for Giovanni. His heart muscle was dying, as was evident from the labs drawn by Dr. Martone.

Shay fell into step beside him.

"That's quite a way to end your shift, with a STEMI."

Dante nodded. "Dr. Martone is an excellent intern and Dr. Fucci will have the block taken care of in no time. When is your shift over?"

"Now. I'm done as well."

Dante cocked an eyebrow. "I don't think we've been off at the same time since we got married three weeks ago."

"You've been working late," Shay said, and then she winced, holding her belly, instantly alarming him.

"Are you okay? Is the baby okay?"

"Yes, I'm just tired." Shay smiled. "I'm fine. I think it's just a Braxton Hicks."

"So early?"

"I'm nineteen weeks pregnant now. Almost halfway there. Braxton Hicks can start in the second trimester."

Dante was going to make her sit down, when a code blue was called from the trauma bay where Mr. Scalzo was. They turned around and walked quickly back to his room.

Mr. Scalzo was unconscious, ashen and in full-blown cardiac arrest. His heart was tachycardia, pumping too fast, and no blood was getting through. There was no blood flow to his brain or other organs. He would be dead soon. Dr. Martone was pumping on the patient's chest hard, trying to get it back into a rhythm, but only the electrical shock would reset the cells of the heart to fall back into rhythm.

"What do we do, Dr. Martone?" Dante shouted over the din as he pulled on gloves.

"Shock the heart back into rhythm and intubate."

Dante nodded and turned to Shay. "Get me an intubation kit."

A defibrillator was primed and wheeled over to the patient. The electrode path was placed on Mr. Scalzo's chest.

"Clear!" Dr. Martone shouted.

They shocked the patient's heart, his muscles twitching as the electricity moved through his body. Now all Dante could do was watch the monitors and wait for the heart, which was now flatlining, to jump back into rhythm.

Come on.

The monitor beeped as a rhythm started.

Shay handed the intubation kit to Dr. Martone while Dante took the man's pulse to confirm that the heart was back in rhythm. Then Dante guided Dr. Martone as he successfully intubated the patient. Once the ventilator was breathing for their patient, Dr. Martone wheeled the patient out of the trauma pod to go up to the cath lab, where Dr. Fucci was waiting. The room cleared and Dante finished his notes, breathing a sigh of relief that the patient wasn't lost.

"Dante…" Shay said, her voice trembling.

"Sì?" He glanced up just in time to see Shay's knees buckle as she crumpled to the floor.

He raced to catch her, his heart hammering. *"Cara,"* he whispered, but she didn't respond. So he scooped her up in his arms and got her to the table.

"Dr. Affini?" a nurse asked as he hit the call button.

"Get Dr. Tucci here now!" he shouted.

Oh, God.

He took her pulse. It was low. And he couldn't help her. He'd lost control over this moment and he hated this loss of control. Hated that he was helpless, that she brought this side out in him in this moment.

He was in danger when he was out of control.

And he didn't like this one bit, but all he could do right now was cradle her.

Protect her.

Protect his child.

Later he could bury the emotions. Right now he couldn't keep them back even if he wanted to. He was only glad that Shay couldn't see him like this.

CHAPTER SEVEN

SHAY STARED UP at the ceiling tile in Dr. Tucci's office, her hands folded around her belly as she took deep calming breaths. She was still feeling a bit shaky, but she felt fine; it was the baby she was worried about now. Dante was sitting next to her, which was a relief, because a moment ago he was pacing.

"You know, Dr. Tucci wasn't even on duty. He was at home," Shay said. "This is very good of him to see me like this. We seem to keep paging him at odd hours. First the paternity test and now this."

Dante just grunted and then got up and paced again. "I thought you were going to make an appointment."

"I did," she countered. "It was for next week. I'm only nineteen weeks, Dante. It's not until I'm in my third trimester that I see an ob-gyn every week. You're a doctor, you should know this."

It was a tease, but Dante didn't take the bait.

He shot her a look of frustration. He dragged a hand through his hair and glanced at the watch on his wrist. It was at that moment that Dr. Tucci walked in.

"*Scuse*, I'm sorry that I took so long," Dr. Tucci said. He saw Dante. "Dr. Affini, I'm surprised to see you here. I thought you were on duty." Dante sat down muttering under his breath.

"I'm the father. Nurse Labadie is now my wife, so I just went off duty."

Dr. Tucci's brows arched at all the answers Dante was giving him, and then he grinned. "Congratulations. I guess I should call you Principessa now."

"You don't need to," Shay said quickly. "In fact, I'd rather not be referred to as that."

Dr. Tucci chuckled and Dante rolled his eyes.

"So what happened, Shay?" Dr. Tucci asked.

"She fainted," Dante said. "Her blood pressure was low. I took it in the emergency department."

Dr. Tucci nodded. "How far along are you?"

"Nineteen weeks," Shay said. "I think I felt a Braxton Hicks."

"I think it's too early," Dante said firmly.

"No, not too early. She's nineteen weeks. They can be felt as early as sixteen weeks. Especially if the mother is tired or under stress." Dr. Tucci shot Dante a knowing look.

Shay couldn't help but laugh. "So it was Braxton Hicks?"

"Well, let's have a listen to the baby's heart." He pulled down the Doppler monitor and lifted Shay's shirt. "The gel will be cold, I'm sorry."

"It's okay. I'm used to it."

Dr. Tucci squirted the gel onto her abdomen and turned on the Doppler. He pressed into her belly and Shay held her breath, waiting to hear that familiar rapid beat of the baby's heart. Dante was frowning and she could see worry etched into his face.

He hadn't heard the baby's heartbeat yet. He hadn't even so much as touched her belly.

Then the familiar thump of the baby's heart sounded on the monitor and Dr. Tucci grinned at her. "Sounds strong, Shay."

She smiled and then glanced over at Dante. The frown of worry was gone and now wonder was spread across his face as he listened to the heartbeat from where he was standing.

"Have you had any bleeding?" Dr. Tucci asked, wiping the gel off her belly with a towel.

"No," Shay answered. "I had some mild cramping."

Dr. Tucci frowned. "The baby's heartbeat is fine, there's no bleeding, so I just think you're overdoing it. Let's check, though."

"How?" Dante asked.

"Ultrasound," Dr. Tucci said. "Just to make sure the baby is doing well and there's no internal bleeding from the placenta. I want to make sure it's intact."

Dante leaned forward, staring intensely at the screen, and Shay couldn't help but smile. He usually was so detached, but this was different. This was nice. He was so concerned about their child in this moment.

Dr. Tucci squirted more gel onto her belly and placed the wand on her belly. The screen lit up and her breath caught in her throat at the grainy image of her child.

Their child.

Dante was beaming as he watched their child and tears stung her eyes at his reaction. Usually he was so guarded, but there was no sign of that now. Perhaps he wasn't as cold as she'd first thought. Maybe she had nothing to really fear and he'd be there for their child.

"No bleeding," Dr. Tucci said.

Dante reached out and gripped her hand, grinning at her as he squeezed it and whispering, "Good."

Dr. Tucci took some measurements and then shut off the machine, wiping her belly again. "You're a nurse with the United World Wide Health Association program, *si*?"

"Yes," Dante grunted, his smile instantly fading. "She's running the simulation training as well as assisting me in the emergency room for the next nine weeks."

Dr. Tucci raised his eyebrows. "You're overdoing it, then."

"I eat small meals. I rest—"

Dr. Tucci shook his head, interrupting her. "You need a couple days to rest. I'm ordering it."

"Good," Dante said. "I'll take her home and make sure she rests."

"I'm on bed rest?" Shay asked, confused.

"No," Dr. Tucci said. "I want you to take three days off, and then you will go on light duty. Only half days. And that's an order."

"Grazie," Dante said. "And thank you for coming in on such short notice."

Dr. Tucci nodded. "I will see you next week and

then for the scheduled ultrasound at twenty-six weeks. We'll make sure everything is still going well and take some more measurements."

"Okay," Shay said, but she wasn't exactly thrilled with the idea of going down to half days. That wasn't in her nature. Work was the only constant thing in her life, except now that it wasn't. What was she going to do with herself?

Dante shook Dr. Tucci's hand and then turned back to her when they were alone. "I'm glad the baby is well and that you're well. That it wasn't serious."

"Me too," she said. She sat up slowly. "Told you it was Braxton Hicks."

"It scared me when you fainted like that."

"I'm glad you were there to catch me." Then she blushed. "I'm okay."

He nodded and took her hand. "You will be. I'm going to take the next three days off as well and I'm going to make sure that you get rest. Proper rest. I'll cook for you and take care of you both."

Warmth spread through her chest. No one had ever taken care of her before. The idea of Dante being there for her was nice.

You can't rely on him always taking care of you. Remember this is just for a short time.

"You don't have to do that."

"I want to do that." He grinned. "Besides, I have some business to attend to in Tuscany and we can spend a couple days at my vineyard. It's quiet there and I think you'll get more rest there than you will here in Venice."

The idea of spending a couple days in Tuscany sounded heavenly, and if she couldn't work, then she was going to do what she always wanted to do, but never found time for, and that was explore.

"That sounds great." Her stomach grumbled and Dante chuckled.

"Let's get back home and get you something to eat. It's still early. We can hit a local bistro on the Lido if you'd like. I think we've both had a long, trying day."

"Now, that's something I can really get on board with." She took his hand as he helped her to her feet.

They grabbed their coats and she had her purse. She informed the other United World Wide Health Association nurses that she was ordered by Dr. Tucci to have three days of rest. She left her simulation training in the capable hands of Danica, who could take over for her because Shay had made up copious notes and prepared the next several simulations.

She and Dante then walked to the ferry pier and caught a ferry to the Lido.

After a short ride, they disembarked.

"The bistro isn't far from here. It's right across the Gran Viale Santa Maria Elisabetta."

"Good, I'm starving."

Dante grinned and took her hand. Just as he'd done in Oahu when they were walking along the beach at sunset. It felt so good, her hand in his large strong one.

"What're you doing?" she asked, shocked that he was holding her hand. She liked it, but she was surprised by it. He'd slung his arm through hers before, but holding her hand was more intimate. And she had to admit she liked it. It made her feel safe.

"For any press lurking around. You are my wife after all," he said, explaining it, and though it made perfect sense she was a bit disappointed in the answer.

What did you expect?

She didn't know and she didn't know why it bothered her so much.

The little bistro faced the Adriatic side and the

warm breeze coming off the water was heavenly. The bistro was filled with tourists from the nearby hotels, but the maître d' found them a table out on the patio underneath lemon trees that were strewn with twinkle lights.

It was perfect and the angel-hair pasta with sun-dried tomatoes was heavenly.

It was delicious.

"You know, you make funny noises when you eat," Dante teased.

"What?"

He grinned, his eyes twinkling as he mimicked the noises she was making, noises that sounded decidedly naughty.

"Making those noises is a compliment."

"*Sì*, I know." He winked at her, grinning.

Her pulse began to race and she thought about the last time he'd looked at her like that and where it had led to.

"Have you been to this bistro a lot?" It was a foolish topic change, but she didn't want to start thinking about the last time they had shared a meal or a drink together so close to a beach.

"*Sì*, I have been here a few times, but never with a woman before if that's what you're getting at."

"No, I'm not." She looked away, knowing that she was blushing.

He winked and took a drink of his red wine, which looked so good, but she couldn't have a drop.

"Oh, I have this for you." Dante reached into his jacket pocket and slid a paper toward her. "It's in English. It's our marriage contract. It outlines our fifty-fifty custody, stipend for living and money for our child. As well as schooling."

Shay nodded as she read it over. The contract benefited her and their child. There was nothing hidden in the contract. It was straightforward.

"Also your visa, *cara*, is taken care of. My attorney arranged for it to be extended indefinitely."

"Indefinitely? I thought our marriage was only for a year."

"We're putting on a show, *cara*."

"Right. Good." She tensed. It all seemed too easy. Why was she uneasy about it?

Because you're having a hard time trusting him.

She didn't know how to trust.

Dante is not your father. He won't abandon our baby.

Shay signed the contract, although her stomach was doing flip-flops.

"Here you go," she said, sliding it back toward him. His fingers brushed hers and sent a jolt of electricity through her.

"Grazie, cara." He took the contract and placed it in his jacket. "Are you okay? Is it Braxton Hicks again?"

"No, I'm just tired." She rubbed her belly and the baby kicked. Hard, for the first time. She smiled, the kick reminding her why she was doing this.

"Is everything okay?" Dante asked again.

"Yes. I think everything is going to be okay."

Dante smiled and then paid the bill. He stood, holding out his hand. "Come, let's go."

Shay took his hand and he led her down to the beach. Her pulse began to race, thundering in her ears. She desired him. She still wanted him, even though she couldn't have him.

Dante affected her so.

They walked along the boardwalk instead of the sandy beach. It was a beautiful night. They didn't say much, but she wasn't worried about the silence between them. It was nice not talking and just enjoying the evening.

"It's a gorgeous night," Dante said.

"It is." She squeezed his hand. "Thanks for being there for me today."

"It's my job. That's our baby you're carrying, *cara*." And the way his dark eyes glowed she forgot for a moment who she was with and how this was only temporary.

She nodded. "Still, I appreciate it. I'm not used to having help."

"I understand." He stopped and tilted her chin so she was staring deep into his dark eyes. "I will be there. I'm here to help you. You can rely on me, *cara*."

And though she wanted to believe him, she was having a hard time letting her heart do just that.

They sped along the winding road that was lined with tall cypress trees. Shay enjoyed the drive in Dante's luxury car. She hadn't even known that he owned a car, until they'd got to the mainland from the ferry and he'd walked her to a car park where the red two-seater was waiting. And she had to say it was a beautiful sports car.

Dante didn't say much on the drive, but she could tell that he was visibly relaxing. He wasn't as tense as he was when he was in Venice. He was smiling to himself the closer they got to Arezzo. Dante's villa was on the outskirts of the city, lying in a valley below the city, but far enough away to enjoy the peace and quiet of the countryside.

"You know," she said, "this is a very nice sports car."

"Grazie." He grinned at her briefly.

"Not very practical, though," she teased.

"What does practicality have to do with it?" he asked.

"There's no backseat—where are we going to put the baby?"

"We?" he asked.

"You." She cursed under her breath for making that assumption. This wasn't a real marriage. There would be no we at all in the near future. Just you or I.

"I can get another car for when I have the baby." He tensed, his knuckles whitening on the steering wheel.

Shay wanted to change the subject. Obviously a touchy matter for him and it annoyed her that she got so upset about it. She knew what she was getting into, but she was so sensitive lately. One moment she could be fine and then next in tears.

"Why don't you tell me a bit about the vineyard?"

"It's been in my mother's family since the seventeen-hundreds."

"Everything in your family is so ancient."

He grinned. "*Sì*, you should've met my Zia Sophia. She was very ancient."

Shay laughed. "I don't think any woman appreciates being referred to as ancient."

"She deserved the title. Enzo and I would make bets on how old she actually was when we were young, because every year she seemed to get younger. I swear her last birthday she was claiming she was younger than me and I was twenty when she passed."

"So how old *was* she?" Shay asked.

"No one knows. There were no birth certificates, but the doctors suspected that she was over a hundred."

"I take it you didn't like her?"

"I adored her. Even if she hid her age. She was young at heart."

"Was she royalty too?"

He shook his head. "No, she was part of my mother's family. I think she was my grandfather's aunt, as he referred to her as Zia Sophia too. What about you? Any elders in your family."

"No."

"No?" he asked, confused.

"Well, there probably was. I wouldn't know. My parents were quite young when they got married and…let's just say their families were extremely religious and didn't approve of a child conceived out of wedlock. My mother was disowned and my father…" She couldn't finish that sentence.

"*Sì?* Your father…?"

Abandoned me.

"My father didn't talk about his family. All I know is the name is Acadian and most of my, I guess, blood relations are in New Orleans, but they didn't want anything to do with us."

Dante frowned. "That's terrible."

She shrugged. "I'm used to it."

"Still, not to know where you come from…"

"I know where I come from. I'm from New Orleans, Louisiana. That's where I'm from." She sighed. She didn't really want to talk about the fact she knew exactly who her family was; she'd seen them. Her mother's parents and siblings.

They were a family of wealth and worth in the Garden District.

And they'd let Shay's mother suffer. They'd let her live in poverty.

And when her mother had died, none of them had come to the funeral. None of them had acknowledged Shay's existence. Frankly, she was better off without them. She'd made do without the traditional family for a long time.

Her baby wouldn't have a traditional family either, but at least he or she would have two parents who cared about them. Two parents who would give him or her all they needed.

Does Dante care?

She wasn't sure. He'd seemed concerned when she'd fainted, fascinated when he'd seen the baby on-screen and relieved when the baby had been deemed well, but she didn't know if it was because of a sense of duty or because he genuinely cared about the baby. He said he wanted to be a father. She still didn't know what was in it for him. He didn't touch her belly, didn't plan for the baby or talk about her pregnancy, other than insisting she marry him.

Yet he was always concerned about her getting her rest, feeding her, making sure she took care of herself. He was taking care of her now in a way no one had before.

That meant he cared, right?

"Ah, we're almost there," Dante announced as they turned off the main road, down a small dirt road that went through a small village. "It won't be long now."

"Oh, good," Shay said. And she enjoyed the sights of the small village as Dante slowly drove through, the dirt road giving way to a cobbled stone street. They went over a narrow stone bridge suspended over a gorge, a river tripping over rocks as it wound its way down the hill the village was on.

As they rounded a small square featuring a tall bell tower on the church, the dirt road dipped again into a valley. And when they turned the corner Shay gasped at the sight of acres of vineyards, stretching as far as the eye could see.

"*Bellissimo*, isn't it?" Dante asked, the pride evident in his voice.

"*Sì,*" Shay said happily.

He turned up a long dusty drive. The name over the gate they drove under read Bellezza Addolorata.

"What does that name mean?" Shay asked.

"It's the name of the wine this vineyard produces. Sorrowful Beauty."

She cocked her eyebrows. "Ooh. Sounds wonderful."

"*Sì*, when you have the baby, we'll celebrate with a wine I've been saving for a special occasion. One my grandfather laid down."

"I look forward to that."

Dante parked in front of the house. When he opened the door to climb out, an older couple came out, smiling. Shay almost wondered if they were his grandparents, but by the looks of them they were too young. She got out of the car as Dante was embracing the couple.

He then turned, grinning, and gestured to her. "*Mia moglie*—Shay."

The woman shouted with happiness and then rushed her. Taking her in her arms and kissing her, while who Shay could only assume was her husband grinned, his hands thrust deep into his pockets.

Shay was bowled over by the woman clinging to her, saying things Shay could not understand but could only interpret as happiness.

"Who is this?" she asked, smiling back at the woman, who had finally let her go.

"This is Zia Serena and Zio Guillermo. Not relatives, but they have worked with my grandfather their entire lives. They're caretakers of the vineyard. Zia Serena took care of my grandmother after my grandfather died. They treat me a bit like a son, since they don't have children of their own."

Zia Serena nodded and then motioned to Guillermo as they marched back into the house.

"Well, the villa is big enough for them to live here."

"They don't live here. They own a house on the other side of the property. I called them and let them know we were coming. Zia Serena made sure the house was stocked. She's made lunch." Dante grinned. "We'll get you fed, and then you can rest in our room while I go inspect the vineyards with Zio."

Shay's stomach did a flip-flop. "Our room?"

He turned around. "Of course. We're married and Zia won't understand that ours is just a marriage of convenience. She's only prepped one room. There's a couch in the room. I can sleep there."

Her pulse pounded in her ears at the thought of sharing a room with him.

Even if he was sleeping on the couch.

She was apprehensive, but honestly she had no one else to blame but herself. She'd decided to sleep with him that night five months ago and she'd agreed to the marriage of convenience.

Dante had forgotten how much he loved sitting around his late grandmother's rough-hewn wooden table in her kitchen. Even though his grandmother had died a few years ago, he could still feel her presence in the brick walls and could still see her rattling the copper pots that swung on the ceiling in the gentle breeze wafting in through the open back door to the garden.

Zia Serena had prepared a light lunch, with a *Caprese* salad and fresh-baked bread. There was *espresso* and *biscotti*. Zia Serena didn't speak a lot of English, but she knew enough to tell Shay to eat and a few stories about Dante when he was young.

Much to Dante's chagrin and Shay's delight.

Once they were done with their food, Zia Serena insisted on cleaning up. Dante made sure that Shay was settled into bed with strict instructions to nap, before he followed Zio Guillermo out the back door and down into the vineyards.

"You've been gone too long," Guillermo remarked.

"I'm a surgeon. I've been busy."

Guillermo just *harrumphed* and then stopped to examine a leaf. "It's good you got married. Your grandfather would be proud."

Dante's stomach knotted when Guillermo mentioned his grandfather.

Would his grandfather be proud of the fact he'd got married only to legitimize the child and keep the land? Essentially his marriage was a sham.

He didn't think his grandfather would be so proud about that. However, the fact Dante was thinking of his child, willing to do whatever to properly raise his child, would make his grandfather proud.

His grandparents had loved each other. When he'd spent summers here, he could see the love between the two of them. Something his parents had never had. Although Dante was sure that his mother had loved his father at some point.

"You know, there were some men here last month with your father," Guillermo said with disdain. Dante knew Serena and Guillermo didn't think much of the man who'd broken his mother's heart. The royal title and status did not impress Serena or Guillermo one bit.

"Oh, yes?" Dante inquired. "What were they here for?"

But deep down he knew.

They were eyeing up the land to sell when Dante's thirty-fifth birthday came at the end of spring and the trust slipped into his father's hands. Thankfully, the marriage put a stop to that, and once the baby was born, then it would all transfer to Dante. And Dante knew that his father was not at all pleased about the prospect.

"Your father was going to sell this vineyard, *sì*?"

Dante nodded. "They came to the Lido villa too, Zio. I sent them away."

And he had. He'd chased them off.

His father had no right to send out Realtors to his property, even if time was running out for Dante to wed and have a child.

Guillermo chuckled and then clapped Dante on the shoulder. "I would've liked to have seen you chase them away. I would've liked to have seen your father's expression."

"He wasn't with them."

His father knew better than to come near Dante.

Dante had made it clear in no uncertain terms that he wanted nothing to do with him.

His father had done enough damage over the years, lying to them, breaking promises.

Guillermo spat on the ground. "He's a coward."

"*Sì*. I couldn't agree with you more." He dragged his hand through his hair. "Show me the rest of the vines you were worried about so we can figure out what's going on."

Guillermo nodded and kept walking on.

Dante trailed behind him, taking it all in, trying to remember everything his grandfather had taught him about the delicate art of winemaking. He glanced back up at the house and saw Shay standing on the terrace in a white summer dress. His heart skipped a beat. She wasn't looking at him; her eyes were closed and her face was tilted up toward the late-afternoon sun. There was a smile on her face and the wind blew back her short blonde locks.

He could see the swell in her belly, the perfect roundness, and his heart swelled with pride. When he'd seen his baby for the first time on the ultrasound, he'd realized that this was more complicated than a simple marriage of convenience.

He liked things simple. Cut and dried, but this was more. Shay was carrying his child.

His child.

She was more than a wife on paper. Inside her was a piece of him.

It wasn't just him alone anymore.

That was his baby inside. The fact that Shay was carrying his flesh and blood made him desire her all the more.

His. Yet he was afraid to think possessively over the baby. To reach out and feel the kicks.

Olivia had made him so wary. He'd been so hurt when he'd found out the baby he'd been hoping for back then wasn't his. She'd shattered all his hopes of a family. Shay promised him an inkling of something more, but he was so afraid to reach out and take it.

She turned back toward the open doors and headed back into the bedroom.

Dante sighed and turned back to the vines.

It was better he kept his distance from Shay. She'd made it clear that she was only doing this for the child's sake. She didn't want him. It was apparent when she was horrified about the idea of staying in the same room as him tonight.

Perhaps I should sleep in the barn?

Only he didn't really ever enjoying sleeping on a bed of hay. Not that there were any animals left in the dilapidated old barn besides field mice and the occasional owl. And he couldn't sleep in the living room. Zia Serena had promised that she would be back up at the house early to cook them breakfast. She'd insisted on cooking all their meals while they were here so Dante could focus on the vines and Shay could rest.

It was dark when Dante returned from the fields with Guillermo. He washed outside with Zio and they both wandered inside, where Dante could smell something he hadn't had the pleasure of tasting in a long time.

"Braciole!" he exclaimed.

Serena grinned and nodded. "Guillermo and I will be out of your hair soon, Dante."

"You can stay for dinner, Zia."

"No, you and your bride must have alone time."

"What's going on?" Shay asked.

"I was trying to convince Zia and Zio to stay, but they refuse."

"Oh, but they must! She cooked this food for us." Shay turned to Serena. "Please stay."

Serena patted her hand but shook her head.

"We'll take our dinner back to our home. Sit, Dante."

Dante took a seat next to Shay while Serena dished up the tender steak stuffed with cheese, bread crumbs and raisins that had been marinated in tomato sauce. *Braciole* was served for special occasions in his house and it was accompanied by pasta and bread so you could soak up the sauce.

"I'll be back tomorrow morning." Serena kissed the top of Dante's head and took a small covered pan with their dinner out of the house. Guillermo waved as he followed the food and his wife.

Now it was just the two of them. And an uneasy tension fell between them. Last night at the bistro and then when they had been walking along the boardwalk, all he could think about was taking her in his arms and kissing her. He could remember the taste of her sweet lips, how she'd trembled in his arms when he'd made love to her.

He had been so close to her and he wanted that closeness again.

Only she'd made it clear she didn't want that. She had been so upset when he'd said he'd extended her visa to longer than one year. As if he were trapping her or something.

"What is *braciole*?" Shay asked. "Don't get me wrong, it looks so good—and smells good too."

"It is delicious. It's steak, pounded thin and stuffed. Then it's cooked in tomato sauce."

Shay cut a piece and took a bite. "Oh, my goodness, that's so good."

"See, I told you." He took a bite and it melted on his tongue. Not as good as his grandmother's, but almost there.

"How were the vines?" Shay asked.

"Healthy. There was a bit of a problem area, but I'll get it fixed. How was your rest?"

"Peaceful." She sighed and then smiled. "I really had a good sleep. I can't remember the last time I slept so well."

"You look beautiful tonight," he said, and it was the truth. He only ever saw her in scrubs. She was still wearing that white dress, but now she was wearing a stylish wrap over her bare shoulders, because it was a bit cool in the evening. It was still spring.

A pink tinge rose in her cheeks. "Thank you."

He wanted to say that she looked as if she belonged here in Tuscany, but he didn't.

"I brought a book to read tomorrow on that terrace." Serena chuckled. "Your Zia Serena was insistent I rest. She wants to bring me my meals when you're in the fields."

Dante chuckled. "Don't try to fight her. She'll win."

"I don't have any intention of doing that." Shay sat back. "That was an amazing supper. And I thought you were a good cook. Serena is just absolutely amazing."

"I'll tell her that," Dante said. "It will make her day."

She smiled. "Well, I think I'm going to head back to bed to rest. I'm not used to eating this heavy this late."

"Farmers have to tend the land until the last drop of light is gone." He stretched. "I'll clean up. Go rest like Dr. Tucci told you to."

"I'll leave a light on." There was a nervous tinge to her voice as she left the table to head upstairs.

"Grazie," he whispered as he watched her head up the back stairs to the bedroom above him. His pulse thundered in his ears. He glanced at the couch in his grandmother's sitting room. It was old, but it was a heck of a lot more inviting than taking a chance with his self-control upstairs.

CHAPTER EIGHT

WHEN SHAY WOKE up in the middle of the night, she expected Dante to be next to her. She'd actually fallen asleep in a curled position so that he'd have lots of room and they wouldn't accidentally touch.

She made her way down the stairs quietly and found that he was sleeping on the very short couch in the sitting room. He looked very uncomfortable and his legs were propped up over the end of the couch.

Her foot creaked on the last stair and he craned his head to look at her. "Shay, what're you doing awake? You're supposed to be resting."

"I woke up and you weren't there," she said. "I thought after the big fuss you made about sharing a room in order to keep up appearances that you'd come up."

Dante sighed. "I thought better of it."

She came down the last step into the living

room. She sat down on an armchair across from the couch. "You don't look very comfortable."

"I'm not," Dante groused. "I remember it being a lot more comfortable when I was younger."

She chuckled softly. "You were probably shorter."

"*Sì*, I was." He laughed and then groaned as he tried to stretch his six-foot frame out.

"I shouldn't have made such a big deal. We're grown-ups. Come upstairs. We can share a king-sized bed." Her heart skipped a bit as the words slipped past her lips.

"Are you sure?" he asked.

"Yes." And she hoped her voice didn't quiver. She stood and held out her hand, hoping it didn't shake. "Come on. If you spend another couple hours on this thing, you won't be able to move in the morning."

He took her hand, making her skin prickle at his touch, and she led him upstairs. "Yes, and if I was limping too much, Zia Serena would insist on using her homemade liniment on my back."

"Is it any good?"

"Yes, but it stings so much and smells so bad."

"I can only imagine."

"I'm not sure you can," Dante teased. "It would curl your hair."

Shay laughed, but she was unfortunately familiar with scents that could curl your toes. She'd been in enough situations where breathing through your mouth was a better solution.

"Come on," she said, changing the subject. "You can stretch out, and then you won't get attacked by Zia Serena tomorrow."

They walked into the bedroom and she crawled back into bed, adjusting the pillows so she could lie on her side, which was the only comfortable way to do it.

Dante opened up the terrace doors to let in fresh air. The moon was high in the sky and bright, casting moonlight against the white bedcover. He padded over to the bed and lay down carefully on his back, with his hands folded behind his head.

"Does the breeze bother you?"

"No," she said. "It's nice. And the moon is so bright."

"*Sì.*"

"I guess that gives credence to that old Dean Martin song."

He grinned at her—she could see his dark eyes twinkling in the moonlight. "Don't sing it."

"Why?"

"I've heard you sing."

She gasped. "When?"

"You sing when you're busy and you've tuned the world out. I've heard you singing in your office and when you're chopping fruit. You sing, but I hate to tell you that you have a terrible singing voice."

Shay hit him with a pillow. "That's not nice!"

"I am only telling the truth, *cara*."

"Oh, and you sing *so* much better?"

Dante rolled over and leaned on one elbow. He began to sing in Italian. A rich, deep baritone that made goose bumps break across her skin. As if he was wooing her in song and it was working. At the end of the song he cocked his eyebrows, as if to say *see, I told you so*, so she hit him again with her pillow.

"And what was that for?" he asked, snatching the pillow from her.

"For upstaging me."

He chuckled. "I'm sorry."

"So how long have you run this vineyard?"

"This is my first year," he said.

"I'm confused. I thought your grandfather died a while ago and left you this vineyard."

"*Sì*, but it was in the family trust until I reached

a certain age." He cleared his throat and looked uncomfortable. "Now I am of age. It is mine."

"Is that why your childhood home was sold?" Shay asked.

"*Sì,*" he said bitterly. He was on his back again, frowning up at the ceiling.

"Was that part of your inheritance?"

"No, that home should belong to Enzo, but father sold it off before our mother died. He's determined to get it back. All I was left was this vineyard and the villa on the Lido di Venezia. That is all I wanted and that makes me happy."

"Are you going to give up surgery for winemaking, then?"

"No, I love being a surgeon. Even more than winemaking. Zio Guillermo is perfectly capable of running the estate while I'm gone."

"Just like a prince," she teased.

"How so?"

"Vassals and serfs to attend to your every whim."

He snorted. "I'm telling you, it's just a title. Prince means nothing in my country."

"It means something to some people."

"People who live too much in the past," he said hotly. "You know, Zia Serena starts breakfast very early. I think we should try to get some sleep. I know that you need your rest."

And with that quick change in demeanor she knew that the conversation was over. There was no use trying to dig further. She'd get nowhere. He was stubborn.

That much she'd come to learn in the short time she'd been with him.

It could be a good quality some of the time, other times it was downright annoying. Just like this time.

Of course, she was no better.

She was just as stubborn too.

That was what her mother always said, but Shay's stubbornness had helped her survive. It had helped her endure her childhood, where she'd often had to parent herself. It'd helped her survive Katrina, natural disasters when working with the United World Wide Health Association and her mother's death.

She was a survivor, and if that meant being stubborn, then so be it.

She was stubborn.

The scent of pancetta frying roused Dante, but it was the thumps to his hand that caused him alarm. As he pried open one eye he saw that his hand was placed on Shay's belly and the thumping was from the resident occupant taking up space in her womb.

It was his baby.

His baby was kicking him. It wasn't very strong, but he could feel it. Like a poke of a finger under a blanket against his palm.

A smile tugged on the corners of his lips.

He wasn't sure how his hand ended up there or why he was spooning Shay, who was still sound asleep, but in that moment he didn't care either.

And he couldn't figure out why he'd been so afraid of this moment, because it was nothing to be scared of. In fact, it made him feel more connected to it all. Perhaps that was why he was always so reluctant to reach out and touch the child growing under Shay's heart: because he was too afraid.

Afraid to feel that deep connection with a child who might be taken away from him.

He snatched his hand away and rolled over.

Shay stirred. "What time is it?"

"It's seven in the morning. Don't get up," he said, sitting up and putting his feet down on the cold tile floor.

"Too late. I have to get up." She got up and padded off toward the bathroom down the hall.

He chuckled and then got ready while she was out of the room so that he was gone before she came back. If she wanted to continue to sleep, he wasn't going to stop her. She needed her rest.

Dr. Tucci had made that clear.

Dante didn't want anything bad to happen to Shay or the baby.

After freshening up in the downstairs bathroom he headed into the kitchen, where Zia Serena was laying out a large breakfast. She didn't even look at him when he entered the room.

"Guillermo is waiting in the fields for you," Serena said. "Eat and then go out and see him."

"Is something wrong, Zia?" Dante asked as she set the plate in front of him. Usually she was all smiles, especially when she was feeding people, but this morning the smile was gone and replaced with a frown of concern.

"Guillermo wasn't feeling too well this morning but still insisted on going to the fields."

"He should stay home," Dante said.

Serena threw her hands up in the air in exasperation. "That's what I told him, but he won't listen to me. Perhaps if you talk to him."

Dante nodded and took a bite of his egg. "How has his angina been?"

"He takes the medication you prescribed for him, but he doesn't always listen to the local doctor's orders."

"That smells so good," Shay said as she came into the kitchen and took a seat.

Serena lit up when she saw her and she made a plate up for Shay.

"What're you going to do today?" Dante asked Shay.

"I don't know. I thought about going for a walk."

"Do you think that's wise?" he asked, frowning.

"Dr. Tucci said to rest, he didn't say anything about complete bed rest, so why can't I go for a walk?"

Serena nodded in agreement with Shay, though she was probably only picking up the odd word. She set the plate down in front of her and went back to the stove.

"This looks so good," Shay said, eagerly eyeing the scrambled egg, pancetta and mounds of fresh fruit.

"Well, if you want to go for a walk, why don't

you come down to the fields with me? I need your second opinion on something."

"I don't know much about winemaking," Shay said. "I'll gladly go for the walk, though."

Dante waited until Zia Serena had left the room and then whispered, "Guillermo has angina."

"Okay," Shay said.

"He's been experiencing some pain and I suspect he's not going to the doctor. He won't let me near him, but maybe if I had a second set of eyes…"

She nodded. "Gotcha. It's something I would often do for the doctors when we were in remote villages. Patients may not trust the doctor but could always trust me and they'd open up to me."

He grinned. "That's what I'm hoping for. Guillermo is a stubborn man."

"Are you sure he's not blood related?" There was a twinkle in her eyes and he couldn't help but laugh a bit as he finished up his breakfast and put the dirty plate in the dishwasher.

Shay finished up and he took the plate from her.

They both donned a pair of wellies because the fields were a bit muddy after a fresh round of fertilization a day before they arrived.

Guillermo wasn't too far from the main house,

which was good because from a few feet away Dante could tell that Guillermo wasn't doing so well.

"He's ashen," Shay whispered. "That's not a good sign."

"I know. Serena said he was complaining of heartburn and was feeling off, but he still insisted on doing his job."

And Dante was fearful that Guillermo, standing right in front of them now, was having a heart attack. And the nearest hospital was Arezzo, which was forty kilometers away.

"*Buongiorno*, how are you feeling this morning, Zio?"

Guillermo waved his hand but didn't answer. Also not a good sign.

Shay moved closer and Guillermo beamed at her, taking her hand. She just smiled at him and walked beside him.

"He's sweating profusely and it's not that hot out yet," Shay said over her shoulder.

"*Cosa ha detto?*" Guillermo asked. What did she say?

"Zio, did you take your angina medications this morning?"

"*Sì*, I did. I always take them, but this morning I'm having a lot of indigestion. My jaw hurts too."

Dante shot Shay a look and she nodded ever so slightly, as if in tune with his thoughts. Guillermo was having a heart attack.

"Guillermo, we need to go to Arezzo." Dante took his arm and Shay the other.

"Why?" he asked, his voice panicked.

"I want to get you looked at. I think it's more than indigestion. The hospital in Arezzo can take care of you."

Guillermo didn't try to fight, and when they got back to the main house Shay got Guillermo to sit down. Dante explained quickly to Serena what he thought was happening. And she took it in her stride, knowing that if she became overwrought it wouldn't keep Guillermo calm.

It wasn't long until an ambulance pulled up the long drive.

Dante explained what was going on with Guillermo. They got Guillermo loaded into the back of the ambulance and Serena climbed in with him to ride to Arezzo.

As the ambulance flicked on its sirens and headed away, Dante sighed. "I'm sorry."

"What for?" Shay asked.

"You were supposed to come here for rest."

"You shouldn't apologize for Zio Guillermo having a heart attack. That's not something you can control."

Dante cursed under his breath. "I should be able to control it. I like control."

"And you're a trauma surgeon?" she asked quizzically. "There's no control in that choice of profession."

He rolled his eyes and she just laughed at him.

"Well, now we have the house to ourselves." He ran his hand through his hair, because he was nervous at the prospect. At least when they were alone in Venice or at the villa on the Lido there were neighbors around. At the vineyard, they were truly alone.

And that terrified him.

Shay walked through the rows of vines, carrying an ice-cold glass of sweet tea for Dante. Dante had retreated to the vineyards after the ambulance left and she hadn't seen hide or hair of him all day. So she'd decided to make a pitcher of sweetened iced tea. Which was no easy feat.

She'd had to scour the kitchen until she'd found a few bags of black tea in the back of a cupboard.

She'd brewed it, strained it and poured it into a pitcher. Adding sugar until it was the right taste that reminded her of summer days when her mother would make sweetened tea for her. Then she'd taken one of the fresh lemons in the big bowl of fruit on the counter and sliced it thinly.

It was the best refreshing drink on a hot day and she could only imagine that Dante was out there sweltering. So she'd poured him a glass and put on her wellies under her long summer dress and headed out into the vineyard. He wasn't far from the house; he was working on the stretch Guillermo had been working on before they'd called the ambulance.

He was crouched down with pruners in his hand, staring at the leaves. His shirt had been abandoned and the late-afternoon sun made his bronzed skin glow like that of an ancient Roman god. The usually tame dark curls were haphazard and beads of sweat ran down his face and his large, muscular biceps.

She hadn't realized how muscular he was, until she saw him out here, working on the vines.

It was as if he were someone totally different, but the same.

Her heart skipped a beat and she couldn't help but admire him.

He was absolutely beautiful.

As if sensing her admiration, he glanced up. "Shay, are you okay?"

She shook her head. "Fine, I thought you might be thirsty."

"Sì." He stood and stretched and she tried not to stare at his half-naked body, because then that would remind her of that stolen night together. The way her hands felt running over his muscles as she clung to him. She handed it to him and he took a drink and then looked confused.

"What is this?" He was frowning.

"Iced tea, or, as we call it, sweet tea. True iced tea is—"

"Just cold tea." He made another face. "I don't like it. I don't like tea."

"What? Why?"

"It was kind of you, but I can't drink this." He handed the glass back to Shay.

"What's wrong with it? Is it too sweet?" She frowned at the cup in her hand, the condensation on the glass making her palm wet.

"I don't like tea."

"Why?"

"It reminds me of being sick."

She arched her brows. "Sick?"

"*Sì*, my mother would always make it for me when I was sick. I don't like tea."

Shay chuckled. "Is that why there was only a small amount in the cupboard?"

He grimaced. "Medicinal use only."

"Well, I tried. I might not be able to cook much, but I pride myself on my sweet tea."

Dante grinned. "Well, if I didn't associate tea with sickness, I'm sure I would enjoy it."

"Ha-ha."

He picked up a towel and wiped off his hands quickly. "Are you hungry, *cara*? Would you like some dinner? We can go into the village."

"That sounds nice."

"Let me just have a quick shower and we can head into the village."

They walked back in silence to the house. Dante had a quick shower and changed into jeans and a white crisp shirt that was unbuttoned at his neck and rolled up on those strong forearms. His curls were tamed once again, but he didn't shave his five-o'clock shadow off. And the bit of stubble suited him. Shay kicked off the cumbersome wellies and put on her sandals.

It was a short drive to the small sleepy village, which was built into the side of a hill and made of cobblestone. Dante found one of the few parking spaces, and then they walked together to the *piazza*, which was in the heart of the village.

A tall clock tower loomed over them and in the center of the *piazza* was a large fountain. The gentle breeze blew mist from the fountain onto them, but it felt good. It was a surprisingly warm day. Humid. Almost as warm as it was in New Orleans in the summer. Which was brutal for humidity.

Shay closed her eyes and she could almost swear she was home, except for everyone around her speaking Italian.

"This way," Dante said, and his hand touched the small of her back as he led them to a small bistro with an outdoor patio with red checkered tablecloths, which was tucked at the corner of the *piazza*.

"Ah, Principe! It's a pleasure to see you again." The maître d' turned to her and grinned. "Is this the Principessa?"

Shay plastered on a fake smile, but her stomach began to twist and turn as she thought about people knowing that she was married to him. She didn't like being in the limelight.

"Sì," Dante said graciously, but she could tell that he was annoyed by the attention too. Which just endeared him to her more.

Don't get attached. This isn't permanent.

"This way," the maître d' said, and he led them to a corner table out on the patio, so they could enjoy the twilight *al fresco* style. He left them with a menu, but Dante ordered for them.

"What did you just order?"

He grinned and winked at her. "You'll see."

"Hmm, well, I suppose I should trust your judgment. You haven't let me down yet."

"Of course, I could be getting you back for that sweet-iced-tea concoction you tried to force down me earlier today."

"I didn't force it down you." She laughed with him.

She liked laughing with him.

It was like the way it used to be. Before she got pregnant. When they didn't have to link their lives together. They'd had fun in Oahu.

Too much fun, remember?

"So tell me about your mother," Dante said softly. "You speak of her and yet you don't."

"She died as a result of Katrina. It's why I joined the United World Wide Health Association. To help those who can't afford health care."

"I'm so sorry, Shay. How did your mother die?" he asked gently.

"The place she stayed at after the floodwaters receded was full of toxic mold, but she couldn't afford to stay anywhere else and she had to stay somewhere while she waited for FEMA to provide housing. She got really sick from the mold, and in the end the toxins overwhelmed her body."

"I'm really sorry." He reached out and placed his large hand over hers. It felt so good.

Be careful.

She cleared her throat. "Now, you tell me about your mother. You don't speak much about her either, but we're staying at her childhood home, yes?"

Dante nodded slowly. "She died a few years back. Cancer."

"I'm so sorry, Dante. That must have been hard to bear."

"Yes. She was a wonderful mother, but…" He trailed off and moved his hand off hers. "My father was difficult. She thought he was her prince and he was far from that."

I hear you.

"My father left my mother," she said. "He said he was going off to Alaska to crab fish and earn the money to bring us all up there. We never heard from him again."

"Did he die in an accident?" Dante asked.

"No, I know he's alive. I know for a fact he is. He just left us."

Dante snorted. "My father didn't leave my mother, not physically at least. That's not what marriage should be about. It shouldn't be a lie."

"I know," she said softly, but he didn't hear her or what she was implying about their own sham marriage.

The waiter brought their food.

"Panzanella," Dante announced. "I figured you wouldn't want to eat anything too heavy in this heat."

"Grazie," Shay said. The salad was filled with pieces of the traditional Tuscan bread, *fettunta*, and mixed with fresh crisp greens, tomatoes, cucumbers and onions. It was melded with olive oil and vinegar. There were also tuna and capers in this version.

It was delicious and, by the kicks she was getting, the baby approved too.

Once they were finished, Shay couldn't have dessert. She was too full. So Dante paid and they walked across the *piazza* in the dwindling light.

"I've enjoyed my time in Tuscany. It's sad that we're leaving tomorrow," she said.

"*Sì*, it's always hard to leave here, but I'm a surgeon and I love that just as passionately too." They stopped by the fountain to watch the water.

"It'll be good to get back to work," Shay said.

"You'll remember to take it easy," Dante warned.

She was going to respond, when she heard a screech and a crash. They both spun around in time to see two cars collide at high speed, flipping one car over and over.

When the cars finally came to a stop, Shay was running behind Dante as they rushed toward the scene.

CHAPTER NINE

SHAY SET UP a triage, as she'd done countless times in the field.

Thankfully, since the paramedics had arrived, she had more access to modern equipment. And these paramedics knew English as well. Which was heaven-sent, so she didn't have to keep getting Dante to translate for her. Though from being in Italy for almost a month now she was picking it up to the point she could be useful in emergency situations.

They had the patients laid out. Shay tagged them by priority, using the colored sticky notes that she always carried around in her purse.

The fire crew that was also on the scene was busy extracting one of the worst victims with the Jaws of Life. The crash scene was a jumble of twisted metal and fumes from the petrol.

Dante was assessing his patient through the wreckage, instructing the fire crew on how to extract him. He was up on the wreckage, aiding the occupant of the car through the broken wind-shield. And she couldn't help but admire him.

He was passionate about medicine. His passion and compassion just made her want him more. If she weren't pregnant, she would be doing the same thing. She'd done the same thing in the past.

Dante and she were so similar.

Only she couldn't help Dante and the driver of that vehicle right now. Instead Shay tended to the young couple who were in the other car, while paramedics helped an elderly man who had been in a third car that was involved in the wreck.

The young man who was being extracted had been going too fast and had lost control when he'd reached down to answer his phone. That was when he'd ploughed into the young couple.

Shay knelt beside them. The young man had a few lacerations, but the paramedics had strapped the young woman down, because she couldn't feel her legs.

"I'm so sorry this happened to you," she murmured as she took her pulse rate.

"You're American?" the young woman gasped. "Oh, thank goodness."

The young man looked at her. "We're here on our honeymoon. Beatrice and Tim O'Toole."

"I'm Nurse Labadie. Shay."

Beatrice sighed with relief. "I'm so glad. I wasn't sure how I could tell these paramedics that I'm… I'm pregnant."

Shay's stomach knotted and she placed a protective hand on her belly. "How far along?"

"Just eight weeks," Tim said. "We really need to know if the baby is okay."

Shay didn't want to say anything to them. The baby was so small, it could still be alive, but if there was damage to Beatrice's spine, then the chances were slim. She didn't want to give them false hope. The only way they would know for sure was by ultrasound.

Tim turned back to the paramedic who was dressing his bandage and getting him to climb onto a gurney to be taken to Arezzo.

"Tim?" Beatrice called out frantically because she couldn't turn her head all the way to see what was happening behind her.

"He's just being put into the ambulance. He's okay."

Beatrice let out a shaky sigh. "We were just married a week ago, but we've been together for a long time."

"How long?" Shay asked as she tended to some minor scratches.

"Since we were sixteen. He's my high-school sweetheart. We've been saving a long time for this trip."

Shay smiled warmly at her. "I'm sorry that this has happened."

"As long as we're both alive and the baby is fine, we can survive anything." There was a tremble on her lips as she talked about the baby and Shay couldn't help but wonder if she was thinking the same thing that Shay was: that the baby was lost. Her hand instinctively cradled her belly. As she did that Beatrice's gaze tracked down.

"You're pregnant?" she said, grinning at her.

"I am. I'm just halfway there."

"A boy or a girl?"

"I don't know. I thought it would be nice to have a surprise!"

"Your husband must be thrilled." Beatrice smiled and then winced.

Yes. Husband.

Thrilled she had right, because Dante seemed to really want this child, but Shay still wasn't used to calling him husband because the marriage wasn't real.

Only she didn't say anything as the paramedics came and got Beatrice, loading her into the ambulance. The moment that she was loaded, Tim leaned over, bandaged up and bleeding, to take her hand. The way Beatrice looked up at him and the way he looked at her made Shay realize that she had never looked at Dante like that and he'd never looked that way at her.

Her mother had looked at her father like that, but he'd never reciprocated.

This was what true love was.

And they might lose their baby.

Shay touched her belly again as the ambulance doors closed and was reminded how life was so unfair. Dante came up behind her. He touched her shoulder. She turned around and saw his shirt was stained with oil and grease, as was his face. He was sweaty and looked tired. Almost beaten down.

"Are you okay?" he asked gently as he brushed her cheek with the backs of his knuckles. It was nice, but she didn't want the comfort. She was okay.

"I'm fine. My patient was pregnant, but only eight weeks along. I hope the baby is okay."

"Me too," Dante said gently.

She turned to see a blanket draped over the wrecked car and a sheet over a body on a gurney and her heart sank. Then she understood the weariness in his eyes.

He'd lost the battle.

"Oh, I'm sorry. You were working so hard." And then she felt bad for rejecting his comfort.

Dante sighed. "There was nothing more I could do. His body was too broken. Once he was extracted, the pressure on his internal bleeding released and he bled to death in seconds. I'm not even sure surgery would've saved him had I been able to open him up right here and now. So much damage."

"Mi scusi, Dottore..."

Shay turned and saw policemen there and she knew that they wanted a statement from him.

"I'll be back as soon as I can, then we'll get you back to the villa so you can have a peaceful sleep before we drive back to Venice tomorrow."

She nodded and he went to speak to the police about the accident. Shay wandered back over to the fountain. There were still a few curious onlookers to the accident and a few people were praying.

She sat down on the ledge of the fountain,

watching Dante speak to the police officer and trying to keep her eyes off the young man whose life had been cut short due to a careless mistake, but, mistake or not, a life had been cut short. Possibly two. And if Beatrice was paralyzed, her life would be changed forever.

A twinge of pain raced across her belly. She sucked in a deep breath as it passed, assuming it must be Braxton Hicks as she had overdone it this evening. She'd spent the last couple of days relaxing and on her last night at Dante's vineyard she'd thrown herself into the fray of her work.

So she was making herself stressed again. She deep-breathed through the pain.

And soon it was gone.

She was mad at herself for not listening to Dr. Tucci and running a small triage in the middle of a *piazza*.

Because that is your true love. Work.

And what else was she supposed to do?

She couldn't leave that young couple there. Broken and in a foreign country. Pregnancy or not, she'd signed up to be a nurse. To help others.

She would continue to take it easy because that was how she could help her baby, but she had to help others too.

Her work was her love. Her reason for living.

And it was the only thing that remained true in her life.

They'd been back in Venice for a few weeks and Dante had been trying to catch up on all the work that had piled up. He knew that Shay had been as well, though most of the paperwork she did from the villa. Ever since they'd left the vineyard she'd been unusually quiet. He knew the easy workload was getting to her and now she was over halfway through her pregnancy.

He thought maybe it had to do with the accident and he thought it would cheer her up to learn that Beatrice's baby had survived and that she wouldn't be paralyzed. There was temporary paralysis, but it would abate and Beatrice would be able to walk again.

All she had said was "That's good."

Then he thought perhaps she was worried about Guillermo. She'd taken such a shine to him. When he gave her a status update on Zia and Zio, how Zio had had a mild heart attack but would recover quickly, she gave the same answer and returned to her paperwork.

He shook his head and flicked through the

stack of mail his maid had left on the kitchen counter of the villa. Mail he had been ignoring because he'd been so busy.

A heavy cream envelope stood out from the rest and he opened it, groaning as soon as he saw the word *masquerade*. It was an invitation to the hospital's annual charity masquerade ball, which would raise money for funding. It was always a huge success. Everyone dressed up in their finest and hid behind Venetian masks.

It was a fancy dress gala along the lines of Venice's most infamous carnival, which was usually held in the winter months. He hated going to these affairs. Anybody who was anybody attended this event. Even heads of state, and as he was technically a head of state he had to attend. Plus he was Head of Trauma and collaborating with the United World Wide Health Association.

It was pretty much mandatory that he be there.

"What's that?" Shay asked as she came into the kitchen carrying an empty bowl.

"An invitation to a gala fund-raiser for the hospital."

"Ooh," Shay said, sounding intrigued and showing more interest than she had in the last weeks, which made him happy. "It sounds fun."

"It's not, but it's for a good cause." He stared at the envelope.

"Well, aren't you going to open it?"

"Should I?" he teased.

"Yes."

He broke open the seal and read it over. "Hmm…"

"Well, when is it?" she asked.

"It's tonight."

"Too late to RSVP?" She sounded disappointed.

"Do you want to go?"

"Not really, but you should."

"I don't want to go." He leaned across the counter. "Why, do you want me out of the house?"

"I don't…" She sighed. "I feel like I'm holding you back. You've been hovering over me like a ticking time bomb since Tuscany. I'm fine and I want you to have fun."

"Trust me, this gala isn't fun."

"Well, if you have to RSVP, then you don't have to go. You could just ignore it."

"No, it's more of a reminder. I go every year." Dante cursed under his breath. "I was hoping to catch up on some paperwork for the simulation program this evening."

"I can do that, you go." She turned her back to him, washing her dish in the sink.

"You're going to do my paperwork?"

"Sure," she said brightly. "Then you can get out instead of watching a pregnant woman sleep."

"You think you're getting off that easy?" he said as he grinned from ear to ear. "You're coming with me."

The bowl clattered in the sink and she spun around. "I'm what?"

"You're my wife." He grinned, enjoying the look of distress on her face. "And you're coming with me."

"Uh, no, I'm not."

"Of course you are. You are a princess. It's your duty." He grinned.

"Duty?" she asked, her voice rising an octave.

"*Sì*, you're coming with me." He pinned the invitation to the corkboard in the kitchen. "You seemed so excited before."

"That's when I thought you were going. I can't go." She ripped the invitation down from the corkboard and handed it back to him.

"Why not?"

"Dante, I don't have anything to wear, for starters." Then she pointed to her belly. "I don't think they make ball gowns for pregnant women."

"Of course they do. There have been pregnant women who have gone to balls before. You're coming." He slapped down the invite and walked out of the kitchen, grinning to himself because he knew full well that she was following him out of the room.

"Dante, I don't go to fancy galas." Her voice was panicked. "I've never been to one."

"Now's your chance." He was really enjoying this.

"You're teasing me."

"Well, I am a bit, but I would like you to accompany me."

"I don't want to go. I should be resting." She jutted out her chin, her pink lips pursed together in defiance.

He laughed out loud. "That's the first time you've used that as an excuse here."

"Well, a gala is… It sounds terrible. I'm not one for crowds. Can't you go by yourself?"

"You are my wife."

She crossed her arms. "I don't even know where to get a dress from. I would call Aubrey, but she's working today. How am I going to find a dress?"

"The Lido has many shops around here. You can go and find a ball gown in one of them. I'm certain."

Her mouth opened and closed a few times, as if she was going to say something, but instead she left the room, calling over her shoulder, "I'll wear what I have, but I'm not going shopping."

"The gala starts at eight. I'll be home at five to get ready, so hopefully you're ready then."

Dante picked up his keys and his briefcase. He was going to have his assistant pick out a dress for Shay and make sure it was delivered in time. She was his wife and he wanted her to feel good. She was beautiful, sexy, and he wanted the world to know it.

When he walked into the Palazzo Flangini tonight with Shay on his arm, he was confirming to the world, and to his father, that he was married. That he had it all.

That he was going to have an heir and his father's chances for getting a hold of his vineyard and the villa were gone. Dante had no doubt that his father would be there tonight with one of his mistresses and he hoped his father heeded his advice from his mother's funeral about not approaching him.

Dante had no interest in mending broken fences with that man. A father in name only. Dante would be a better father than his ever was. A better husband too, for as long as Shay would have him.

Tonight he wasn't just wearing a Venetian mask, he was wearing a different mask. One of a loving husband and father. He had to show the world that Dante Affini was happily married. And maybe then people would leave him alone.

His marriage had put an end to all that talk about the trust fund and his father's cheating. It was bad enough his mother had suffered through all those stories in the paper about his father stepping out with different women.

All Dante wanted, all he'd ever wanted, was a quiet life.

Was that too much to ask for?

The box containing the most beautiful black lace ball gown arrived at lunchtime with a note from Dante that asked her to take the ferry into Venice and then catch a *vaporetto* to the Palazzo Flangini on the Grand Canal. He also sent a Venetian mask on a handle; white, painted with black and silver filigrees.

It reminded her of Mardi Gras in New Orleans.

The only difference was that usually involved beads and bright colors such as purple and green.

This was more elegant, more sophisticated, and she was terrified. She doubted anyone would be flashing their boobs for beads tonight. She'd never done that, just as she'd never been to a gala before. She hadn't even gone to her own high-school prom. She was so worried about making a bad impression and embarrassing Dante. So she really wished that she weren't going. She was clumsy and awkward, even more so being pregnant.

However, the dress was stunning. As were the matching shoes, which were thankfully small kitten heels, and jewelry. He'd thought of everything. Except that he wouldn't be escorting her. She had to make her own way to the gala.

Dante had apologized in the note, explaining that he had to work late on a trauma case that had come in, but he promised to meet her there.

"How will I even know who he is if everyone is wearing masks?" she mumbled, looking up from the note while sitting cross-legged on his bed, and Dante's cleaning lady overheard her.

"He'll be wearing a matching mask. That's how

it's done. His will be more masculine, though."
Maria, the cleaning lady, patted her shoulder.

"Thanks, Maria."

Maria nodded and continued her cleaning of the en suite bathroom.

Shay stared at the gown again.

She really didn't want to go, but she didn't want to let Dante down either. And it could be good to mix and mingle with those who might donate to the United World Wide Health Association. Dante wanted this marriage of convenience. He was giving up a lot to be part of his child's life. So the least she could do was play the part.

Ever since they'd got back from Tuscany she had been a little standoffish with him because she'd thought it was for the best, but she'd been so lonely. Especially since she was on modified duties and everyone else she knew was busy with their own jobs.

She hated this feeling of helplessness she'd been experiencing lately.

She missed her work. She hated being on light duty.

She missed being in the emergency room, triaging, teaching. She missed being a nurse.

Pretending to be a wife tonight was something

not very high on her list of priorities, but maybe tonight she could make connections. Tell more people about the good work that the United World Wide Health Association did.

At least that way she was doing something. She glanced at the clock. She had three hours to get ready and head over to the Palazzo Flangini.

Once Maria was done with the bathroom, Shay took over and had a shower. Her hair was a short stacked bob, so she added some curls with her curling iron, pulled on the beautiful lace dress and did her makeup. By the time she was ready, it was time to catch the ferry from the pier to Venice.

Maria walked out with her, locking up, so Shay wouldn't have to worry about wrecking her dress trying to latch an ancient iron gate.

As she walked down the main road on the Lido to the pier there were a few curious onlookers. Especially since she was carrying a Venetian mask, but she tuned them out as she boarded the ferry, just before it left. Once she disembarked at the Venice pier, she found the water taxi that could take her down the Grand Canal to the famous Palazzo Flangini, where they held the Venice Carnivale every February.

It was getting dark and the canal was lit up. There were many water taxis vying for the water entrance to the palace. Once she was at the entrance, she was helped up out of the water taxi and showed the doorman Dante's invitation. She followed the crowds inside, holding the mask up to her face as they walked into the main room, where the gala was being held. Except it wasn't one big room, but different rooms. The walls were covered with Renaissance artwork, the ceilings were gilt and there were lots of marble columns.

People in the party filtered around from room to room, chatting, and Shay didn't know how she was going to find Dante in this mess of people.

She kept to the outside of the flow of people wandering around the *palazzo*. Until a tall man in a designer tuxedo, holding a more masculine mask with the same markings, approached her. He moved through the crowd easily. They parted for him as the Red Sea parted for Moses. His presence seemed to command it so.

"Ciao, cara."

Her heart skipped a beat. She recognized his voice and he moved the mask off his face to bring her hand to his lips, kissing her knuckles, which made her stomach flutter.

This is just a show. It's all just a show.

Only it was fooling her, this show she kept re-iterating she was acting through. Her heart fluttered and the baby kicked in response to her accelerated pulse rate.

She moved aside the mask. "You look very handsome."

He grinned. "You are absolutely stunning."

Warmth flooded her cheeks and she covered her face again. The mask was coming in handy for that.

"You're too kind."

"I'm not being kind. It's the truth." He leaned over and whispered in her ear. "You're glowing, *cara*, and I find it absolutely sexy."

A shiver of anticipation ran down her spine as he took her arm and led her away from the safety of the wall out into the mix.

"Thank you for the dress," she said. "It's wonderful. I don't feel like a beached whale in this."

"Since when have you looked like a beached whale?" he asked.

"Since this bump is getting bigger," she teased.

He chuckled. "You're beautiful. Radiant."

She blushed again. They moved through the social circles. Shay shook hands with a lot of people whom she couldn't speak to, but she knew that Dante was talking up their simulation program and that was all that mattered. They finally moved to a room that was full of art being auctioned off as part of the fund-raiser. The room was also thankfully mostly devoid of the crush of people, which was good because she was getting hot.

And she was exhausted by socializing with a language barrier.

"My father is supposed to be here," Dante groused. "I haven't seen him."

"And that's…?"

"Good." Dante squeezed her hand. "He likes these events. I don't. I didn't want to see him tonight, but then with you here and our baby…well, I was hoping to run into him."

"I take it my presence won't make him happy?"

"No."

"Why?" she asked, confused.

"Because he never wants me to be happy."

Her heart skipped a beat. "And you're…happy?"

"*Sì*, right now, I am."

She gasped and her pulse raced. She wanted

to tell him she was happy around him too, but couldn't.

"I'm tired, Dante."

"We'll go soon, *cara*. I know you're tired."

"Thank you." She held the mask at her side and didn't look at the contemporary art that was on sale, but the Renaissance craftsmanship that was carved into the post and lintels of the *palazzo*. She ran her hand over it and she got a secret thrill of delight touching something that was so old.

"It's beautiful, isn't it?" Dante asked.

"Yes, it is. You know, Venice in some ways reminds me a bit of New Orleans."

Dante arched a brow. "How so?"

"It's close to the water. We also have canals, though not as many as you."

"Go on," he urged, smiling at her, those dark eyes twinkling. Her knees went a bit weak because the suit he was wearing fit him like a glove. It was all she could do to tear her eyes from him.

"We have Mardi Gras and you have Carnivale," she said.

"I think that's the Catholic influence," he teased.

"Perhaps, but I doubt Venice has voodoo roots."

"I don't think so."

She grinned. "So one difference."

"What else is the same?"

"I've seen plantations, on the inside, with similar architecture."

"Wasn't that the Neoclassical movement?"

"Could be," Shay said. "I wouldn't know. I didn't take history, remember?"

He shook his head. "I shall have to school you on history."

"No, thanks." And they laughed together. Her pulse was racing, they were so close, and she was fighting the urge to reach up and kiss him. "Should we make that last round?"

He sighed.

Was that disappointment?

"*Sì*, let's…" He trailed off as he stared over her shoulder. Shay turned to see what had caught his attention. It was a tall, beautiful Italian woman all dressed in red.

She was absolutely stunning.

"Do you know her?" Shay asked.

"*Sì*," he said, through gritted teeth. If he'd been a dog, Shay would have sworn his hackles would be raised as he glared at the woman.

The woman, as if sensing she was being glared

at, turned and looked at them standing at the other end of the corridor.

"Dante?" the woman asked as she glided over to them. "I thought that was you, *mi amore*."

Mi amore? My love?

Dread knotted her stomach and for the first time in her life a flare of jealousy rose in her as the stunning woman called Dante her love and touched his arm as a lover would. She was relieved to see that Dante was none too thrilled to be in the woman's company and did not return the endearment.

"Olivia," Dante acknowledged gruffly. "I thought hospital functions were beneath you?"

"Usually, but a carnival-inspired one sounded too chic to pass up. Besides, Max wanted to come. His hotel chain is donating a vast quantity of money to the United World Wide Health Association." Olivia's cold olive-colored eyes landed on Shay. Her gaze raked her up and down, judging her and looking at her as if she were a piece of dirt. "I see you're not alone either, *mi amore.* Who is this?"

"Shay," she said awkwardly. "I'm a nurse with the organization that you donated money to."

Olivia snickered. "*I* didn't donate. My Max did."

"Well, then, remind me to thank Max," Shay snapped, instantly detesting this woman.

"Bringing a nurse to a society function, *mi amore*. How classless."

"Why? She has every right to be here, and Shay also happens to be my wife—Principessa Affini." Dante smiled down at her, with pride on his face, the way Tim had beamed down at Beatrice when they were in the back of the ambulance. Shay's heart swelled and she held on to Dante's arm.

"Your…your wife?" Olivia asked, stunned.

Dante grinned at her, but it was cold. Calculating. It made Shay shudder, and then he reached down and touched her belly, the first time he'd ever done that.

"We're having a baby." Dante took her hand and kissed it. "We're so happy. Aren't we, *cara*?"

"Yes," Shay said breathlessly. Her heart skipped a beat. Maybe he did want more. Maybe this wasn't like her parents' marriage. Maybe it was real and she was just too blind to see it. Why *couldn't* they be happy?

Olivia smiled, but it was forced. "Well, I see you got what you always wanted. A little nobody who will bear your fruit and drudge beside you in that sham of a hospital."

"Don't you dare speak about my wife like that. You have no right!" Dante growled, and a few people nearby stopped their chatter and looked. The last thing Dante would want was the press to hear about this and report on it. Shay knew how much he detested any publicity.

"Dante, it's okay." Shay tugged on his arm. "She's not worth it."

"You're right, *cara*. She's not. Good evening, Olivia." He grabbed Shay's hand and led her in the opposite direction, out of the corridor. She could barely keep up with his pace as he weaved through the crowds. Once they were at the exit, Dante waved down a water taxi. His face was like thunder as he helped her down into the boat and gave the captain strict instructions to the Lido as he climbed on board and sat next to her.

"Is everything okay?" Shay asked.

"Fine." Dante scrubbed his hand over his face. "I'm sorry Olivia said those things to you. She's mean and spiteful."

"It's okay, but I have to agree with you there."

"No, it's not okay. You're my wife. It's most definitely not okay."

"Who was she?"

"A former acquaintance." He turned to her. "She means nothing to me. You mean so much more to me, *cara*."

Tears stung her eyes and he slipped his arm around her and held her close.

Shay wanted to believe him, because he meant so much to her too.

CHAPTER TEN

THE LAST THING Dante wanted Shay to know about was his past with Olivia, but when he saw Olivia at the gala he'd become so angry. The way Olivia had looked down on Shay had angered him. No, it'd infuriated him.

His fight-or-flight instinct had kicked in and he'd wanted to fight.

And now he was angry at himself for engaging with Olivia. For not walking away and for her showing up and spoiling a magical night.

And it *was* a magical night. Shay looked so stunning in that dress. The moment he'd seen her standing off to the side, pregnant with his child, his first thought had been *She's mine*.

When he'd seen her there, he'd no longer wanted to be at that gala. He'd wanted to take her home and take that dress off her. He'd wanted to hold her in his arms and kiss her. She'd never looked so beautiful before.

He'd wanted her so badly, but he'd known they

had a duty to do and he wasn't sure if she wanted him the same way that he wanted her. So he'd tamped down his ardor, but it had been so hard, and then Olivia had shown up, angering him. Directing pointed barbs at Shay, who was a thousand times a better woman than Olivia ever was, and he couldn't help but wonder what he'd seen in Olivia in the first place. They were polar opposites in personality. Shay was caring, kind and Olivia was self-centered and selfish.

The ride home in the water taxi was silent.

Shay didn't press him with any more questions.

Which was a relief. If she pressed him, he'd lose control and it wouldn't take much. His grasp on the reins of his emotions were wearing thin.

He didn't want to get into it. He didn't want Shay to know about his secret shame. The way he'd been duped by Olivia.

Once they were back at the villa, though, she made him a cup of espresso and sat down at the table with him.

"Tell me about Olivia," she said gently.

He shrugged. "There is not much to tell. She's a former acquaintance. We had a falling-out years ago."

"Obviously there's something. It was like you'd seen a ghost. You two were lovers?"

"We were. Long ago. It's not important." Dante loosened his bow tie and unbuttoned his collar.

"How long ago?"

"Long." He cursed under his breath. She deserved to know the truth, but he didn't want to talk about Olivia. "I don't want to discuss it, *cara*. It's a painful memory best left in the past."

"Okay. I'm sorry."

"You have nothing to be sorry about, *cara*. It's my fault."

"How?"

"For getting involved with a woman like her. She's a user," he said bitterly. "She wanted to be with me because I was a prince. She just wanted to be a princess."

"Ah, so that's why she seemed so ticked when you referred to me as your Princess."

"*Sì*, it was a dig." He sighed. "You see, not many people knew I was a prince until my father started selling off Affini land and real estate. Then it was outed that there were two Affini men who were bachelors, set to inherit a vast fortune. She wanted in, so she took advantage. That's why I get so angry seeing her."

Shay's eyebrows rose when he said vast and he braced himself for the fact that she would ask how much was vast, but she didn't ask him that. It was as if she didn't care about his money, but he found that hard to believe. Most women he met in his circles cared only about money and status.

Whereas Shay seemed to care most about helping those who couldn't help themselves. Even though Shay had admitted she came from the poorest of the poor in New Orleans, money wasn't what attracted her. Doing good and being passionate about saving people's lives was what mattered to Shay.

And he couldn't help but admire that; but he still wasn't sure that he could trust her.

He wasn't sure that he could ever open his heart up again.

And he hated himself for that. For being so hard-hearted.

"I'm sorry she hurt you so bad."

Dante cursed under his breath. "*Sì*, I was hurt, but I'm angry that she showed up tonight. And that she treated you so badly."

"I'm okay. She can't get to me. I've heard worse. Although it killed me that she's so beautiful and tall. Elegant."

Dante brushed his hand across her cheek. "You are more beautiful, *cara*."

She deserved so much better than him.

Shay placed her hand on his shoulder, rubbing it and trying to console him in that sweet, simple way she did.

She was an angel.

He'd forgotten.

He smiled down at her. And then he touched the swell, where their baby was, and her eyes filled with tears. "I'm happy. What I told her was true. I'm happy about the baby."

"You've never... You've never touched the baby before," she whispered as she placed her hand over his. "I liked when you did earlier at the gala and I like it now."

"I have felt the baby, but you were asleep when I did." The baby pushed back. A strong kick against his palm. Last time it was a tiny poke.

"This baby takes after its daddy, that's for sure—he kicks me enough to annoy me," she said, trying to make light, and he chuckled.

"I know," he said, and he tilted her chin to make her look up at him. Those beautiful dark eyes of hers, those soft pink lips—he'd forgotten how truly beautiful she was. He leaned in and kissed her. It was as if he were tasting ambrosia. He wanted more and he knew that if he pursued this further one kiss would never be enough.

"Dante," she whispered against his lips. "What're we doing?"

He didn't respond; instead he scooped her up in his arms and kissed her again. "I believe I'm taking you upstairs, *cara*."

Shay didn't say no, instead she kissed him back, those long slender fingers of hers brushing the hair at the nape of his neck as he carried her up the stairs to his bedroom. He'd never made love to a pregnant woman before and he wanted to be careful with her.

He didn't want to hurt her.

And most of all, he wanted to take his time.

He set her down on the floor and cupped her face to kiss her again. He couldn't get enough of her kisses. He undid the zipper in the back and helped her out of the black lace dress while she kicked off her shoes. The dress pooled at her feet as he kissed her neck, knowing how that spot had made her moan with pleasure before.

She let out a sigh, her arms wrapped around him as he trailed his hands down her bare back, undoing her strapless bra. Her hands undid the buttons to his shirt and slipped inside.

He loved the feel of her hands on his chest. Those soft, delicate hands.

Shay finished undoing the buttons of his dress shirt. Then he shrugged himself out of his jacket and let her peel off his shirt.

"I've missed you," she whispered as he held her close.

"*Sì, cara.* I've missed you too."

She led him to the bed and sat down on the edge as she guided him down with her. They sat on the bed, kissing and touching. Just as they had that night in Hawaii. Only this time it wasn't the sounds of the Pacific Ocean and palm trees swaying outside the bedroom, but the sounds of the Lido at night. Of a cruise ship blaring a horn as it came close to the lagoon.

It was the night sounds of Venice, but he drowned them all out, because all he wanted to hear tonight was Shay, moaning in pleasure and calling out his name.

Shay hadn't expected the kiss, but she didn't stop it because she wanted more than anything to be with him. She wanted that kiss. For just one brief moment she wanted to be happy.

To remember a time when she had thrown caution to the wind and experienced real passion. To that one perfect night.

Even if that one perfect night had led to an unplanned pregnancy and them being in this situation now. She'd always sworn to herself that she didn't want to have a sham marriage and she should push Dante away. Only she couldn't.

Right now, she wanted to feel.

To taste passion one more time.

His mouth opened against hers as she kissed him, his kiss deepening. His hands were hot on her bare back, holding her tight against him. And then he pushed her down on the mattress, lying beside her.

She'd never wanted someone as badly as she did Dante.

Even though they'd been apart for months, that hadn't changed. And she'd known that the moment she'd laid eyes on him that day in the hospital.

She desired Dante above all other men.

She *craved* him and that thought scared her

because she knew he didn't feel the same about her. She was treading a dangerous path.

The kiss ended and she could barely catch her breath, her body quivering with desire. He trailed his hands over her body.

"Shay," he whispered. "I've missed you."

He wanted her, just as much as she wanted him. A tingle of anticipation ran through her. She remembered his touch, the way he felt inside her, the way he made her feel when she came around him.

No words were needed, because she knew they both wanted the same thing.

"So beautiful," he murmured, pressing a kiss on her shoulder. His hands skimmed over her again.

When he kissed her again, it was urgent against her lips as he drew her body tight against his. Their bodies pressed together and warmth spread through her veins, then his lips moved from her mouth down her body to her breasts.

She gasped in surprise at the sensation of his tongue on her nipple. Her body arched against his mouth and the pleasure it brought her, her body even more sensitive to his touch thanks to the pregnancy hormones.

"I want you, so much," she said, and she was surprised that she'd said the words out loud, but it was the truth.

Dante kissed her and she was lost, melting into him. "I'll be gentle, *cara*. Please tell me if I hurt you or the baby. I don't want that."

"You won't hurt me. I just want to be with you again, Dante."

He stroked her cheek and kissed her again, his hand trailing down over her abdomen and then lower. Touching her intimately. Her body thrummed with desire. She arched her body against his fingers, craving more. Wanting him.

Their gazes locked as he entered her. He was murmuring words in Italian, just as he'd done before, and that made a tear slip from her eye.

"I'm sorry," he whispered. "Did I hurt you?"

"No, I'm just remembering. Good things." She kissed him. "Don't stop. Please don't stop."

"I won't." He nipped at her neck and began to move gently. Slowly. He was taking his time. She wrapped her arms around him to hold him close as he made love to her. He kissed her again and then trailed his kisses down her neck to her collarbone. It made her body arch and she wanted more of him. She wanted him deeper and she wrapped her legs around his waist, begging him to stay close, but she couldn't get him as close as her body craved, because of her belly.

"*Cara*, let me help you," he whispered as he rolled her onto her side. He helped lift her leg and entered her from behind, her leg draped over his. His hand on her breast as he made love to her.

Her body felt alive. She had never thought a feeling like this would be possible. She had never thought that she would ever get to experience it again with him.

Even though her relationship with Dante was not real and had an expiration date, she couldn't help but care about him. Deeply.

Maybe love?

She shook that thought away. There was no room in her life for love. Just her work, just her baby.

Their baby.

And this moment.

She wanted to savor it. He quickened his pace and she came, crying out as the heady pleasure flooded through her veins. Dante soon followed and then gently eased her leg down. She rolled onto her other side to look at him.

Dante was on his back, his eyes closed. She slid

close to him and laid her head against his chest. He slung his arm around her, his fingers making little circles on the bare skin of her back.

"*Cara*, that was…"

"I know," she said.

He kissed the top of her head and held her close. She didn't want to leave this bed. She didn't want to leave his side. And that thought terrified her.

She was just like her mother.

Shay was falling in love with a man who didn't love her back. A man who'd married her because there was a baby on the way.

Only she couldn't let that happen.

She wouldn't spend her life pining for a man who didn't want her.

She had to put a stop to this. To bury her emotions in her work.

Only she was so comfortable in his arms that soon she forgot about all her worries and fell into a deep, blissful slumber.

CHAPTER ELEVEN

SHAY WOKE UP in Dante's arms. As she had every day for the last week. And every day she kept telling herself this couldn't happen again.

She was weak, and he only had to whisper *cara* and she melted into his arms.

Not that it was strange to wake up beside him. She was getting used to it. During their couple of nights in Tuscany she had slept beside him and that hadn't fazed her one bit. And now, for the past seven days she'd enjoyed waking up in his arms. His breath on her neck as he slept.

It was almost natural, as if she were meant to wake up beside him.

And with that came the truth that she could no longer deny: that she was deeply in love with Dante.

Maybe always had been, and she was mad at herself for falling in love with him. She'd promised herself that she wouldn't fall in love with someone unless they reciprocated it. Sure, Dante lusted after her, but did he love her?

She didn't think so. Yet the way he'd been so protective of her last week at that gala, the way he'd told her that he was happy, the way he'd made love to her every night gave her hope. And that was scary.

She couldn't trust hope.

She slid out of bed and quietly got ready for the day. Just as she had when she'd first moved in with Dante and headed to the hospital to run a triage simulation set in the mountains.

Today was a day that she could be at the hospital and it was the perfect place to hide. Which was why she was here setting up a triage situation.

Tarps? *Check.*

Rope? *Check.*

She went over her list on her computer pad as she laid out all the equipment. She had ten different patients in the form of mannequins who were all suffering from various ailments, but as she stared at the checklist on her computer pad she couldn't think about the various trauma that she could be facing during a volcanic eruption.

All she could think about was her own personal

volcanic eruption that had happened last night. Thoughts of Dante and his lovemaking were taking over her every waking moment.

This was exactly what she didn't want to happen.

He was starting to invade every part of her. And on cue their baby kicked as if to remind her that was true.

She glanced up at the projector screen where she'd posted the levels of triage as it pertained to assessing people in the field for care. Especially when there were mass casualties involved. And a natural disaster such as a volcanic eruption or a flood, among other things, could bring in a lot of casualties.

She'd seen a volcanic eruption when she'd been working in the southern part of Mexico. A volcano had erupted and the lahar not only killed hundreds of people, but injured hundreds more. They'd had everything from broken bones, to impalement, infections from the lahar's mud getting into open wounds and dry drowning.

In cases where many were hurt, she'd learned a useful tip from the US Army about dividing casualties into Immediate, Delayed, Minimal and Expectant.

Each of the mannequins fell into those categories, and if the trainees had been listening, they should be able to figure out what dummy fit into what category.

"Shay?"

She turned around to see Dante, dressed in his scrubs and white lab coat, standing in the door of the room where she was running the triage simulation.

"Yes, how can I help you?"

"You left very early this morning," he said as he shut the door behind him.

"Well, I was anxious to get this simulation set up." She didn't look at him; if she looked at him too long, she'd succumb to his charms again. She'd throw herself into his arms and beg to stay with him.

And that wasn't what she wanted.

Her career path was with the United World Wide Health Association. When her time was up here, she'd travel on to somewhere new, once her baby was old enough to travel with her. Of course, she would be doing training and teaching jobs in cities as opposed to dangerous field-work. There wasn't really any permanence to her job, a place to make roots, whereas Dante was settled here.

He had land here. He had roots.

He would never ever leave Italy. She knew that.

How could they ever even conceive of being together?

"Shay, about last night…"

"No, we don't need to talk about last night. It was wonderful, but I get it. It was one time. Of course, every time we sleep together we remind ourselves it's only one time and then fall back into bed together. We have to stop. We've breached the terms of our marriage contract. It has to stop."

It was harsh, but she had to put an end to it to protect herself. She had to put an end to it before she got too carried away.

A strange look passed on his face briefly. "Yes. One time."

"Is that all?" she asked, trying to ignore the fact that he'd moved up behind her. Last night when he'd come up behind her, he'd been buried inside her. And her blood heated as she thought of that intimate embrace. His hand cupping her breast, his kisses on her neck as he whispered sweet nothings in her ear.

"I guess," he said. He sounded disappointed. "Do you need help with setting up the triage?"

"No, I'm good." What she needed to do was get him out of this room before the trainees came in and saw her lip-locked with Dr. Affini.

"I can help. You're supposed to take it easy."

"I'm good," she said. Then she smiled at him. She had such a hard time resisting him, but she had to. She couldn't let this go any further. It was a marriage of convenience, not a real marriage.

It wasn't permanent. Just like everything else in her life.

He liked control and she thrived on flux and change.

How could a marriage work with two individuals so different?

No, it was better this way.

"What time is your appointment with Dr. Tucci?" Dante asked and she could hear the frustration in his tone.

"Four o'clock. It's the ultrasound. Do you still want to be there?"

He nodded. "*Sì*, I will be there. I will escort you up there myself if you don't show up in time."

Shay rolled her eyes. "Well, if you would let me get to this simulation, then the sooner it can be done and the faster I can get up to Dr. Tucci's appointment."

"Fine. I will see you here at three fifty-five."

"Unless a trauma comes in?" she asked.

"Correct."

Shay breathed a sigh of relief that he was gone and didn't seem to be bothered by the fact that she was brushing him off. Which just firmed her belief that these feelings she had for him were one-sided.

And that nothing would come of this marriage, other than that her baby would have his surname and have his or her father in their life.

When he'd reached out for her this morning, she hadn't been there. For the past few mornings she'd been in bed beside him, but this time she wasn't, and he'd panicked.

Dante didn't know what to think about that. Only that he'd expected she would be there.

Part of him was relieved that she wasn't, but the other part of him was hurt that she'd left. *What did you expect?*

He didn't know.

Yes. You know.

Only he didn't want to admit to it, because he

didn't believe in it. Sure, there were people who could find happiness, but he wasn't sure that he was one of them. He turned back to look in the room where she was teaching the nursing trainees about mass casualty triage.

A smile tugged on the corners of his lips.

They'd come from such different backgrounds. Shay was so strong. She never gave up and he admired her fortitude. It was what he was attracted to when they'd met at that conference. She didn't give a damn about what others thought of her; he wished he had an ounce of that.

Only it bothered him seeing his name and his family's name splashed over the front pages because of his father's exploits. How the world knew everything about his family and how he couldn't even go for a cup of coffee without the paparazzi lurking around the corner.

He hated it.

And that was why he tried to keep a low profile wherever he went. Why he didn't want to make a fuss, but Shay was so strong. She just jumped into the fray.

She'd been thrust into poverty as a child and he hadn't wanted for anything.

Except love.

He shook that thought away.

Love was not for him. Affini men were notoriously a bunch of womanizers.

You're not. Your mother's father wasn't.

"Dr. Affini, there's someone in a trauma pod who is insisting you attend to his stitches," Dr. Carlo, one of the interns, said as he ran up to him.

"You know how to deal with unruly patients, Dr. Carlo. I don't need to see him."

Dr. Carlo frowned. "I tried all the tactics you've been teaching us to deal with difficult patients, but this man is insistent and he's bleeding profusely."

Dante groaned. "Take me to him."

Dr. Carlo nodded and they walked to the emergency room. There was a small trauma bay that was used for lacerations that was far off from the larger trauma bays that were for patients who were in distress. Patients that needed a large team surrounding them to save a life.

Dr. Carlo handed him the electronic chart and the name that popped up caused Dante to take a pause. Marco Affini.

No.

He hadn't seen his father in years, save for pictures splashed across the headlines.

Dante had had his solicitor tell his father that he was married and a baby was on the way, because Dante couldn't stand the thought of talking to the man again.

Even when he turned in his marriage certificate to stop the process of his father having his inheritance, his father would have wanted to speak to him about the mistake he was making and Dante wouldn't have anything to do with him.

Now he was here. In Dante's emergency room. His father had his back to him, but Dante could see the arm laid out on a tray; a nurse was still cleaning the deep wound on his forearm. There were bloody towels in the trash bins. He'd had a significant blood loss.

"You can leave, Nurse. I can take care of this patient." Dante clenched his fist.

His father turned then. "Ah, look who has finally decided to come pay his respects."

The nurse peeled off her gloves and slipped out of the trauma bay, as did Dr. Carlo. Dante shut the door.

"You were giving my interns a hard time, I

hear," Dante said, setting the chart down and peeling off his white lab coat, before slipping on a trauma gown and gloves.

"Is all that gear necessary?" his father asked in a snarky tone.

"Yes, this is standard protocol."

"I'm your father. The same blood runs through our veins."

Dante snorted. "That's debatable."

His father glared at him. "What is your problem?"

"My problem is that you wouldn't let my intern do his job. How else is he going to learn?" Dante snapped as he sat on the rolling stool in front of his father and began to finish cleaning the wound the nurse had started on.

"I don't want some student stitching me up. I'd rather have you," his father groused.

Dante rolled his eyes and continued to clean the laceration. He was trying to tune his father out.

"I didn't get to congratulate you personally on your marriage." His father's voice was laced with sarcasm.

Dante snorted. "As if you actually *wanted* to congratulate me. You were just angry that you couldn't get a hold of Nonno's vineyard or the Lido villa. Or my money."

"You still have to produce an heir," his father said.

"Shay's already pregnant. Congratulations, Nonno," Dante said scathingly.

His father's face paled, his mouth opening and closing like a fish out of water. "Pregnant?"

"*Sì.*"

"Are you sure it's your child this time? Does she know about Olivia and that child that you believed was yours but wasn't?" His father was clearly relishing digging at Dante's old wounds.

Dante glared at him and then injected freezing into the cut, causing his father to curse. It took every ounce of strength not to jam the needle in hard, but he was a doctor and he would never jeopardize his career because his father was making him angry.

He got up and discarded the needle in the hazardous material receptacle. "So how did this happen? Did the current girlfriend discover you in bed with another woman?"

Marco sneered. "No, I was in a minor altercation."

Dante shook his head. "You're unbelievable.

You know that? Why are you here? You didn't need to have me stitch up your wound. Are you here to torment me because I took away your opportunity to sell Nonno's vineyard off to the highest bidder?"

"What're you talking about?"

Dante leaned over him. "I know. I know that you've had investors out there poking around. I know that big company wanted Nonno's wine under their wing. I know that you've been waiting like a caged animal, waiting to sell it. And now you can't."

"You think you know me so well? You don't."

"So you've come here to make amends?" Dante asked sarcastically.

"No," Marco said. "I came here to meet your bride."

"To find out whether there was an heir on the way."

His father turned and wouldn't look at him.

Dante just shook his head and opened a stitch kit. He began to close his father's wound. Angry that he'd had to deal with his father today. Angry that his father was so unchanged.

So ignorant, so greedy.

He would never be like him. He could never be like him.

"You'll need to stay here until the effects of the painkillers wear off. Sit back and relax and I'll send an intern to discharge you." Dante peeled off his gloves.

"You shouldn't have got married," his father said. "You're an Affini. We're not faithful."

Dante glared at him. "I may be an Affini, but I'm not like you at all."

With that, he left the room.

His father would never change. He would never accept the blame for what he did to Dante and Enzo's mother. For what he did to them.

And for that Dante would never forgive him.

And he would never forget.

Shay was lying on the bed waiting for the ultrasound.

More important, she was waiting for Dante to show up, but he was forty minutes late to her appointment. She'd had him paged, but he wasn't answering.

Which was unlike him. Even if he were tied up with a trauma, surely he'd have found a way to get a message to her?

"Are we still waiting?" Dr. Tucci asked, coming into the room.

"No, he's probably stuck with a trauma."

Dr. Tucci nodded. "Yes, it's always hard for an emergency room doctor to make appointments."

"I'm sure it's the same for an obstetrician," she teased.

Dr. Tucci grinned and tapped the side of his nose as he rolled the ultrasound machine over. "I could've tried to wait another ten minutes, but I do have a consult in about twenty minutes that will now be pushed back."

"I'm sorry about that," Shay apologized. "Usually he would get some message to me about why he was late."

Would he? Do you know him that well?

She shook that thought from her head.

"It's okay, Principessa." He grinned and lifted her shirt, tucking a paper towel just under her breasts, and Shay tucked a towel into the waist of her scrub pants, which she had pulled down. "This will be cold."

The gel squeezed out of the bottle with a little spurt of air and he turned on the monitor. She turned her head toward the screen. She closed her eyes and took a deep breath as Dr. Tucci placed pressure against her abdomen.

"Ah, there is Baby."

Shay looked at the monitor and she could see the outline of her baby, moving, the flicker of a heartbeat and the string of pearls that represented the spine.

Her heart stopped for a moment and her eyes filled with tears as she stared at her baby.

Little hands and a tiny nose and she couldn't wait to see him or her in person and hold them.

I'll take care of you.

"Do you want to know the sex?" Dr. Tucci asked as he moved the ultrasound wand over her belly.

"You know?"

"Well, I have a pretty good idea. It's not one hundred percent factual, but this baby is in pretty good position to show me." Dr. Tucci grinned. "Or shall we wait for Dr. Affini?"

"No, I'll tell him later." If he couldn't be here, then she'd tell him herself. "I'll only tell Dante if he wants to know."

Dr. Tucci nodded. "It's a girl."

A tear slipped out of her eye and rolled down

her cheek; she wiped it away with the back of her hand. "A girl?"

"Sì," Dr. Tucci said happily as he continued to tap the keyboard, taking measurements.

Shay's heart overflowed with love. It was the first time since the stick had turned blue that she'd felt a real motherly connection. Probably because she was so focused on her work. So focused on keeping everything in her life the same, but nothing was the same anymore.

Nothing could be the same.

This little girl was her whole world.

"There, all done." Dr. Tucci wiped the ultrasound gel from her belly. "I'll email you the pictures of the baby. All looks good for twenty-six weeks."

"Thank you."

Dr. Tucci nodded and left the exam room.

Shay cleaned herself up. It was sad that Dante hadn't been here to see it, to share this moment, but his demeanor had changed when she'd reminded him that their marriage was a business arrangement.

I need to find him.

She left the exam room and headed down to the emergency department. She checked the updated chart and saw that Dr. Affini was in the far trauma bay. She headed down the hall and entered the room.

Only Dante wasn't there. Just an older gentleman, clad in expensive designer clothes, who had obviously been treated for a laceration to his forearm, because it was bandaged and there were blood-soaked towels in the trash.

"I'm sorry," she said. "I didn't mean to walk in on you."

He smiled and there was something familiar about the way he smiled, but his eyes were cold. He was a handsome older man, but there was no warmth about him, which gave her a bad feeling.

"You're not interrupting at all." His gaze raked her body up and down, eyeing the belly and frowning in disappointment. "Have you come to discharge me?"

"No, who is your doctor? I can check to see if they have the orders up."

"Dr. Dante Affini," the man said in a weird tone. "He's my son and I know he's anxious to get rid of me."

So that was why she'd seen the Affini name on the chart.

"You're Dante's father?"

He narrowed his eyes. "Yes. I'm Marco and you must be the blushing bride."

"Yes. I'm Shay."

"And that's my grandchild, is it?" He snorted. "Or is it someone else's?"

"The child is Dante's," Shay said, instantly detesting him. "What're you implying?"

"He didn't tell you?" There was a pleased glint to the man's eyes. "Olivia."

"What about her?"

"He was engaged to her and she was pregnant, with what he thought was his child, but of course it wasn't. What a huge blow to his ego."

"I'm not Olivia," Shay snapped. "I would never do such a thing."

"Even for wealth?"

"Money is not important to me."

"I find that hard to believe." He leaned forward. "Money is power."

"Money is not everything." She didn't like Dante's father at all and now she understood why he didn't like his father much either.

"Then why did you marry him?"

"To give my child a father."

Marco snorted. "Do you know why he married you?"

"For our child."

He shook his head. "For money."

"I don't have any money. I work for the United World Wide Health Association. I'm not in it for the money. Your son helps people as well and he doesn't get paid astronomical amounts."

Marco grinned deviously. "He didn't tell you?"

"Tell me what?" Her stomach twisted in a knot. She didn't like the way this conversation was going; she should just leave, but she couldn't move.

"He only married you to keep his trust fund. Dante and his brother have to marry by the time they're thirty-five and produce an heir from that marriage in order to keep their inheritance. If they don't, then they lose it all. It goes back to me. All their mother's dowry, which she left in trust to those boys, becomes mine again."

Her heart was crushed. She knew there was a reason why he'd been so insistent that they marry, but she didn't want to believe it.

She wanted to believe better about him.

"Shay, your father will come back. I believe in him. He's a better man than you give him credit for."

It was the douse of cold water she needed.

She fled Marco's room, tears threatening to spill.

She had to find Dante.

She had to find out if it was true, or whether his father was just being cruel.

Only deep down a little voice told her what she already knew.

And she was angry at herself for letting her guard down.

CHAPTER TWELVE

"I'VE BEEN TRYING to get a hold of you for days. Where have you been?" Dante asked as Enzo answered his phone.

"Working," Enzo said quickly, and Dante sensed there was something more going on, but he didn't have time to pry at the moment. "What do you need, Dante?"

"Father came into the emergency room with a laceration to his right forearm."

There was silence on the other end. Then Enzo cleared his throat. "Are you okay?"

"I'm fine."

"Are you sure?"

"I said the last things I needed to say to him." Dante snorted. "He's not changed one bit, has he?"

"I don't think that he'll ever change, to be honest." Enzo sighed. "How did he get the laceration?"

"I never did find out. All he said was that it was

a minor altercation," Dante said. "I just stitched him up. He told me my marriage is doomed and I left. I'll have to go back and discharge him soon. Especially before Shay runs into him."

Enzo was quiet on the other end. "He said your marriage was doomed?"

"He's not wrong," Dante said. "He said all Affini men were doomed."

"Damned might be more appropriate," Enzo groused.

Dante grunted in response. "I have to find Shay. I have to tell her about the trust fund and Olivia."

"I already know," she said.

Dante spun around to see Shay standing in the doorway, her eyes moist with unshed tears and her arms crossed. "I have to go, Enzo." And he disconnected the call.

"It's true?" she asked, coming into the room and shutting the door behind her.

"What were you told?"

"Your father told me that you married me only to keep your trust fund from reverting to your father. You married me because the baby guaranteed that the money, the land would be yours. And he filled me in on your exact acquaintance with Olivia, but that doesn't bother me. I'm not like her and I'm sorry if you think that I was when I first showed up. I understand your distrust."

"You met my father?" He scrubbed a hand over his face. "I'm sorry you had to meet him."

"He wasn't exactly pleasant," Shay said. "And didn't seem too thrilled about the prospect of the baby. Of course, now I know why. You're taking money out of his pocket."

"Is that what he told you?" Dante asked.

"Are you denying it?"

"No, but we need to talk about this calmly. For the baby."

"Calmly?" she asked, tears in her eyes. It hurt his heart knowing that this was hurting her. He didn't want her to get worked up. She was too fragile.

"Shay…" He tried to hold her, but she moved away from him.

"Tell me," she said.

It's for the best. Tell her the truth.

"*Sì.* That is why I married you. It's my thirty-fifth birthday soon and our marriage put a stop to my father taking away the vineyard and the Lido villa until an heir, our baby, was born."

She shook her head. "Why did you hide this

from me? Why didn't you tell me about this before?"

"Would you have married me?"

"No. Probably not." She sighed. "My parents were forced to get married and my mother loved my father. Dearly, but he didn't return those feelings. It broke her heart. She just pined for him until the day she died. I don't want that. I never want that."

"Well, why did you marry me, then?" he asked. "Did you think that this could possibly lead to something more? You reminded me yourself just this morning that this is a business arrangement."

Shay winced as if she'd been slapped and he regretted the choice of words.

"I want my baby to know their father," she said, her voice shaking. "I thought you…"

"Thought what?" Dante asked, trying to stay calm to keep her calm.

"I don't know," she said quietly.

"Then why are you angry for my reasons?"

"Because you don't want this child. Not for the reasons I thought you did."

"And for what reasons did you think I wanted this child?" he snapped. "You show up here pregnant, my one-night stand. What am I supposed to think? I've been used before, people after my money. People after my title."

"I don't want any of those things," she said. "I never have. I'm not Olivia."

"I find that hard to believe. You grew up with nothing. You've probably been dreaming of a knight in shining armor to take you away. To save you. Well, I'm not him."

Shay glared at him. "I know you're not him. I'm painfully aware of that fact."

"So now you know the truth," he said in exasperation. "The reason I wanted you to enter into a marriage of convenience with me for a year. I thought you understood the parameters to our marriage. Everything was laid out in the contract. I thought you understood that it couldn't go further than this. I thought you didn't want more, but I was wrong. You want more than I can give you."

"I wish you would have told me the reason why you wanted the marriage." Shay couldn't even look him in the eye. "This is why…marriage just doesn't work. Unless both people love each other. It just… It can't work."

"I can't give you anything more," he repeated.

"I don't want more." A tear slid down her cheek, but she held her head up high.

"Are you going to ask for an annulment?"

She shook her head. "No, I won't let you lose your property. Especially to that man. I signed a contract. I'll stay your wife. You'll give my baby a name, but when my twelve weeks' contract is up I'm leaving."

"You can't leave," he said, but he felt terrible.

"Then give me a reason to stay," she said.

Only he couldn't, because he was too afraid.

He was a horrible human being.

Why did he have to hurt her?

Because it's for the best?

Only he wasn't so sure about that.

"I'd better go," she said. "I'm going to pack and move back to the United World Wide Health Association quarters."

"What?" He stepped in front of her. "You don't have to do that."

"What's the point of staying at the Lido?"

"We have to keep up at least the pretense of being married. If you move back into the United World Wide Health Association quarters, then people will know that our marriage is a sham or on the rocks and my father will put things in motion to take back the land."

"What does it matter?" she snapped. "I'm not going to divorce you and the baby will be born. Who cares what the press thinks? Who cares what people think?"

"I do! I care. It's my family name, but you wouldn't understand about family, would you, since your own father didn't want you?"

The sting of her hand slapping him burned, but he deserved it.

She pushed past him out into the hall and he stood there, holding his face. The feel of her palm still burned into his flesh and in that moment he realized his father had been right. He was exactly like him.

It had been two weeks since their fallout and it still tormented her. He never came back to the villa. She lived there alone and, even though she was used to being alone, without him it was lonely. She missed his arms around her at night, and then she was angry at herself for shedding tears over Dante. For missing him, when he clearly didn't want her.

What did you expect? Love?

She'd thought he was different. She'd hoped he was different, but he wasn't. He was exactly the same.

The same as his father, the same as her father. So she made up her mind. Her twelve weeks were done. She was going to leave and head back to New Orleans. The place she always returned to. The only home she knew, even if it wasn't much of one.

Shay leaned against the wall, fighting the tears that were threatening to fall, and she cursed herself inwardly for letting herself fall in love with a man like her father. Something she'd always sworn she wouldn't do, but she'd done it. And she realized that she was just like her mother.

The only difference was that she wasn't going to pine away.

She was going to keep working.

She was going to make damn sure that she forgot about Dante Affini.

How can you forget about him when you carry a piece of him inside you?

Now she had to get up the courage to find him and tell him she was leaving. Contract or not, she was going back to New Orleans. Her baby wouldn't be used as a pawn for a trust fund. A sharp pain stabbed her just under her navel and she cried out. She was getting too worked up. She was supposed to be taking it easy.

Part of her wished that she'd just headed to the Lido instead of trying to find Dante. If she'd headed back to the Lido after the run-in with his father, then she wouldn't have heard from Dante's own lips the real reasons why he'd married her. Wouldn't have had it confirmed that he thought so little about her and the baby. That he'd just wanted the baby because the baby would ensure his inheritance.

Nothing more.

He didn't love the baby and she realized that she would be giving her baby the same kind of father she grew up with. It truly was all about business.

The pain hit again and she doubled over; her heart began to race. She was dizzy and she felt as if she was going to be sick.

It's stress. Just stress. You have a flight tomorrow you have to catch.

Only the pain hit once again, with a lightening of her belly, and she knew it was something more than just Braxton Hicks. She slid down the wall, crying as the pain overtook her body. She was down a hallway that wasn't busy in the evening. A hall that was filled with offices that were closed. She was alone.

Oh, God. Don't let my baby die.

"Shay? Oh, God, *cara...*"

She rolled her head to look down the hall. She could see Dante running toward her and, even though her heart had been broken by him, she'd never been so happy to see him.

He was kneeling beside her. "What's wrong?"

"Pain" was the only word she could pant through the pain racking her body. The world was spinning and she brought her hand up from where she had been clutching her lower belly. There was bright red fresh blood on her palm.

"Oh, no," she whispered. Red fresh blood was never a good sign in a pregnant woman.

She was only twenty-eight weeks along. It was too early to have her baby.

"Oh, God, *cara*, you're bleeding." She was scooped up into his arms. He was holding her close. "We'll get you help, Shay. Please stay with me."

"It's too soon, Dante. Please help our baby. Please."

She gripped the lapel of his white jacket, holding tight to him as her body attacked her. Shay knew what was going on: she was in premature labor. She'd seen it so many times in Third World countries. And if she was bleeding, that didn't bode well for her or the baby.

Her labor was progressing so fast. Why was it happening to her? Was it punishment for entering into this sham of a marriage?

She had just seen Dr. Tucci two weeks ago.

All she wanted was for her baby to live. She couldn't care less about herself. Her baby had to survive. Her baby needed a chance at life.

Dante carried her into the trauma bay. The largest trauma bay and she buried her head in his neck while the pain coursed through her body. She was scared that he'd brought her here. The largest room was saved for the direst situations. How did she go from being normal and healthy to critical?

"Help. Me."

"I know, *cara*. I know." Dante set her down on the examination table. "Someone page Dr. Tucci to Trauma, *stat*!"

He held her hand as the trauma nurses and residents began to fill the room.

As she stared up at him she found herself slipping away from him. In more than one way.

"Shay, please stay with me."

She turned her head away as the nurses slipped on the oxygen mask. She couldn't look at him. He was concerned only because the death of the baby meant that he would lose everything. All his land, his money.

He didn't deserve to be in this room with her, but she couldn't tell him to leave either, because he was the only familiar thing in this room. She didn't like being on the other side of a trauma as she took deep breaths and tried to fight the urge to slip off.

Dr. Tucci came bursting into the room.

"I'll be back," Dante whispered in her ear. He went to speak to Dr. Tucci.

Shay tried to focus on what they were saying, but she couldn't. Instead she closed her eyes and listened to the heart-rate monitor that they had on her belly. The baby's heart rate was speeding up, but it was still there.

Her baby was still alive for the moment.

"We have to get her into an operating theatre now," Dr. Tucci shouted above the din. "Dr. Affini, you have to leave. She's your wife. You can't be in there with her."

"Husbands go into the operating theatre all the time when their wives have C-sections."

"I don't want… I don't want him in there," she managed to say from beneath the mask.

Dr. Tucci nodded at her. "Dr. Affini, please leave the bay."

Dante looked back at her, but she looked away.

If he only wanted their baby for monetary reasons, then he had no right to be here with her while she was losing it. He had no right to share in the pain she was feeling.

"Shay, we're going to put you under general anesthesia. It's safer for you both. We have to move fast," Dr. Tucci said. "Do I have your consent?"

Shay nodded. "Yes. Please save us."

And that was the last thing she could remember before the world went black.

CHAPTER THIRTEEN

ALL DANTE COULD do was watch the clock on the wall. That was all his mind would let him do, because he couldn't let his mind wander to where it wanted to go. He couldn't let it wander to down the hall where Dr. Tucci was trying to save Shay's and his baby's lives. It crushed his heart that he had pushed her away.

That he'd hurt her. Those two weeks apart had made him regret his harsh words.

All he could think about was earning her love back again and not knowing how, but he was going to try. Without her…his world spun out of control. It was colorless. There was no light. No sun.

And the way he'd hurt her to protect his heart sickened him.

That he was like his father.

You're not your father.

He hid his face in his hands and tried to shake all the thoughts away. All those dark thoughts that were niggling away in the dark recesses of his mind.

The one that stuck out the most was that he'd failed Shay and the baby.

He'd absolutely failed them.

Don't let them die.

It was a silent plea, but one that he was hoping wouldn't fall on deaf ears.

Not today.

Lives were saved every day and he wanted to be there when Shay's life was saved, because that was all he had to cling to at this moment.

Dr. Tucci came out of the surgical hall. Still in his scrubs. The grim expression on his face made Dante want to scream; his heart sank into the soles of his feet. Further. Into the depths of absolute despair as Dr. Tucci approached him.

"Please," Dante whispered. "Please don't tell me… Don't tell me she's gone. Please."

Dr. Tucci sighed. "She survived, and so did the baby, but it's not good. Shay lost a lot of blood. A lot. We hung a lot of packed cells."

"What happened?" Dante asked.

"Placental abruption." Dr. Tucci ran a hand over his bald head. "We never know when they're going to happen. It can happen so fast. Just be thankful that it happened here in the hospital and we were able to get the baby out. Usually, by the time the women get here the baby has suffocated and the mother has bled to death."

Dante felt dizzy and he sat back down. His head in his hands, his eyes stinging from unshed tears that would not come.

Dr. Tucci sat beside him and patted his back. "The baby will be fine. She's strong."

Dante glanced up at him. "She?"

"Yes, I forgot you missed the last ultrasound. You have a little girl. She's very small, but already she's a fighter. Ideally we'd have started on steroids in utero to help mature her lungs, but obviously in this case there wasn't time. We have her hooked up to oxygen and various drips to support her while she continues to grow. Of course, you know that she'll have to stay in the NICU until she gains to what should have been close to her birth weight. We also don't let premature babies go home until they're close to their original due date."

Dante nodded. "I know. Thank you, Dr. Tucci."

"We're not out of the woods either, yet, with respect to the Principessa. The damage to her uterus was extensive. The placental abruption ripped through the wall of her uterus. It was a full uterine abruption. I had to perform an emergency hysterectomy. Shay will not carry any more children."

Dante nodded again.

Dr. Tucci left.

This is all my fault.

He was the one who'd got her pregnant and then broken her heart.

He was no better than his father. All because he was afraid of letting someone else in.

Dante left the waiting room and wandered up to the NICU. The nurse on duty pointed him in the direction of the incubator where a tiny baby weighing no more than a couple of pounds was hooked up to a bunch of machines that were helping her live.

He was scared to approach the incubator. He was afraid of what he was going to see. And he wasn't sure that he was ready for this. That he was ready for a daughter.

This is what you wanted, remember? Before Olivia crushed your hopes and dreams.

All he'd ever wanted when he was young was a family. Not that he didn't love Enzo or his mother, but he wanted some sense of normalcy.

He'd wanted that family with a mother, father and child. A loving family who would celebrate holidays together.

Just as his mother had with his *nonno* and *nonna*.

They had loved each other.

All of them.

And that was what he'd always craved when he was younger.

He took a step toward the incubator and looked in to see his daughter. His beautiful daughter. She was so small and fragile. A tear slid down his face as he looked at her.

And he knew in that moment what he was.

He was a father.

This was his child.

"Can I touch her?" he asked the nurse.

"Of course," she said.

Dante put on hand sanitizer and the nurse opened one of the little portal doors to the incubator. He slid his hand in and rested it on her back. There was downy fine hair on her skin. The lanugo she'd never shed because she was born premature.

She was warm, but under the palm of his hand

where she fit so well he could feel her chest going up and down. And the small flutter of her heart.

His baby.

His child.

His future.

Dante slipped his hand out of the incubator and left the NICU. He went up to the ICU, where he gowned and masked to go see Shay, who was still receiving a blood transfusion and still not awake. She was still under anesthesia, in an induced coma while they monitored her.

When he walked into the ICU room, he cried out at the sight of her. She was so pale against the crisp white hospital sheets. She was ashen.

Oh, God.

He'd been responsible for this.

The woman he loved had almost died. The realization hit him hard and it wasn't the realization that he loved her, it was the fact that he'd allowed himself to say that to himself for the first time without hesitation. Without conjecture.

He was in love with her. It was more than a marriage of convenience. It was real. She was his everything.

And it didn't matter to him about his inheritance or the trust fund. If he couldn't have her or the baby in his life, if they didn't get their chance to be a family, then life was not worth living for him. He would give up everything, his pride, his family name, everything that he'd thought he wanted, to have a chance with Shay.

To do things right. To be a real family.

"I'm sorry, *cara*. I will make things right. I promise."

Dante left the ICU room and knew exactly what he had to do. He couldn't be selfish anymore. As he left the intensive care unit floor and passed through the waiting room he saw that his father was here. Two visits in two weeks was more than he'd seen Marco Affini in the last five years and it was two too many.

Dante couldn't figure out why his father was back, but he was unwelcome.

His father turned as if sensing him there.

"What're you doing here? Why did you come back?" Dante asked.

"To see if the child survived. There was a lot of press. Word got out that Principessa Affini almost died. That she was hanging on by a thread."

"It's not any of your business and you know the press always gets things wrong."

"Were they wrong?"

"No, but it still doesn't concern you."

"I think it does," Marco said. "Well, did they live?"

"Do you care?"

Marco shrugged. "It would be a shame, but no, not really. Not for the reasons you think I should care."

"*Sì*, they both survived. So you can go now."

"I think I'll wait."

Dante clenched his fist. "Waiting around to pick at the bones?"

Marco snorted. "Hardly. I actually wanted to wish you a happy birthday. Today is your birthday, is it not?"

"I'm surprised you remembered."

"You're my son," Marco said.

"You've never remembered before now. Or was it because today happens to be my thirty-fifth birthday? Today's the day you could've had it all." It was a dig and Dante didn't care. He deserved it. "And now none of it's for you. You lost it."

"It could still be mine. I hear the baby is sick and that your wife is unable to bear any more children. If your baby dies, then that's it. Unless you leave *this* wife and find another you can breed with."

Dante resisted the urge to pummel his father in the waiting room. "I would gladly lose it all for Shay. If our baby doesn't survive, I will stay with Shay. I love her. I won't abandon her like you abandoned my mother."

"I loved your mother, Dante. It's just that Affini men aren't faithful. My father wasn't, nor his father before him..."

"I *am* faithful. I have always been faithful and I will continue to be faithful. I am an Affini and I am faithful. I am more of a man than you ever were or will be. Now, if you have nothing further to say to me, then I think this is where we part company."

Dante's pulse was thundering between his ears. He was reaching out to give his father a chance.

His father sighed and then nodded. "Good luck."

Dante shook his head as he watched his father leave.

He watched the last of a long line of Affini cheaters walk out of his life forever, because his father was going to be the last of the Affini men to be unfaithful. He wasn't going to follow in his footsteps and Enzo had no plans to settle down. Ever.

He briefly mourned the loss of his father. For the father he could've been, but Marco Affini was weak. Dante refused to be weak.

He was going to fight for what he wanted.

He was going to be strong like the person he loved and admired the most.

He was going to be strong like Shay.

His wife.

CHAPTER FOURTEEN

I'M THIRSTY.

That was Shay's first thought as she started to come out of the anesthetic. The groggy fog that compelled her to keep sleeping, but the more she struggled to stay asleep in that warm, hazy, pain-free cocoon, the more she became aware of her surroundings.

And most important, the fact that she was no longer pregnant.

She let out a small cry.

I've lost her. My baby.

And she began to weep. She wanted her mother there to console her. To ease the pain. Her whole childhood she'd been the balm to ease her mother's pain when she was sobbing over her father. Now she needed her mother's arms to wrap around her and hold her close.

To ease the heart-wrenching pain that was tearing away at her very soul.

The baby she would never get to see.

A nurse rushed in, speaking Italian to her, trying to get Shay to calm down, but she couldn't stop the sobs from racking her body, because nothing could bring back her baby.

"I'll take care of her," a deep, gentle voice said.

Shay turned her head to see Dante standing beside her bedside. He was in his scrubs, but they were wrinkled and she noticed the cot in the corner.

He'd been sleeping here?

She glanced back over at Dante, who was issuing instructions to the nurse, who was nodding and then left the room. It was just Dante and her.

There was no baby.

There was nothing for them.

"What...?" She trailed off because she couldn't even finish the sentence. It was too painful.

"She's alive," Dante said. Then smiled. "Our daughter's alive, beautiful and in the NICU."

Tears streaked down her face. "I thought I'd lost her."

"No, *cara*. You didn't lose her. It was I who almost lost you..." He took her hand and kissed it, tears pouring down his face. "I almost lost you."

"What do you mean?"

"Your placenta abrupted, and it was so forceful it caused your uterus to do the same. It was a full uterine rupture. You almost died."

"Oh, God," she whispered.

"They had to remove your uterus to save your life. You needed several units of packed cells. You almost died. I'm so sorry, Shay. I'm devastated that you won't be able to carry another child. I'm so truly sorry, *cara*."

Tears streamed down her face.

"I'm so sorry," she whispered.

"No, never apologize," Dante said. "Never. You're alive and our daughter is alive. There is nothing to apologize for."

"What does it matter to you? You don't love me." Shay tried to take her hand away. "You have your heir. You don't need me anymore."

"You're wrong. I need you, *cara*." He kissed her hand again. "I love you more than anything. Our two weeks apart were torture. You are my world. I am nothing without you, *cara*."

"How can you love me? You only married me for the baby…" She started to weep but shrugged him away when he touched her. "You only wanted me for the baby, so you can keep your inheritance. You have that. Don't you want someone else who can give you more children? You wanted a family, to be a father."

"You're sounding like my father," he said sternly. "Besides, I am a father.

"You're being cruel."

"You're talking nonsense." He reached for her hand. "I love you, Shay. I was terrified, yes, and my heart was broken and I couldn't trust that emotion. Love was dead inside me until you came along. I don't care if I lose everything by being with you. I love you. I love you, *mi amore*. You're all that I need. You're all that I want."

"You love me?"

"*Sì*, I would give it all up for you. Only you, and if our child hadn't made it, I would still want you. Almost losing you was too much to bear. You are my heart. My soul. My everything."

"You weren't the only fool, Dante. I was a fool too." Shay sighed. "I was so afraid of falling in love and having to give up everything I knew. Giving up my career for a man. I didn't want to be my mother. I was trying so hard not to be her, when I was turning into her."

Dante chuckled. "I understand. I was trying so hard not to be my father I was doing the same. I was turning into him. The only difference in our situations is that you loved your mother. You miss your mother. My father and I, there is no love lost. All we share is a genetic link. We are not the same."

"I am very glad for that."

Dante smiled and then leaned over and kissed her. "I'm afraid I tore up that contract."

"Our marriage contract?"

He nodded. "I want you for more than just a year. I want you for a lifetime."

Shay began to cry again and he kissed her.

"Are you ready to see your daughter now?"

"Yes."

Dante called the nurse, who brought in a wheelchair. He helped Shay into the wheelchair and made sure she was comfortable. He wheeled her down to the NICU, and when they entered that room full of incubators her heart skipped a beat. Dante wheeled her over to the incubator across the room. He lifted the pink blanket and inside was a tiny baby on a ventilator.

Her little girl was so small and fragile. She was hooked up and there were many lines and leads on her tiny pink body, but Shay knew instinctively this was her baby.

"She's so small." She began to weep, not being

able to hold in the emotions any longer. She'd thought she'd lost everything when she woke up. She'd thought she was waking up into some kind of nightmare, but instead she was waking up to a dream that she never wanted to end.

A dream she didn't even know she wanted until she thought it was all lost.

That it was all gone.

Dante opened the incubator and with the help of the NICU nurse they lifted the tiny baby girl from the incubator to place her on her mother's chest. Shay's heart overflowed with a love she hadn't even known was possible. A blanket was wrapped around her little girl and Shay placed her hand over the tiny round back, holding her close.

"It's okay," she whispered. "I'm here and so are you. I haven't left you."

Dante placed a hand over hers. "We're both here now, *mi amore*. And we're not leaving."

The familiar little heartbeat thrumming against her calmed Shay and the baby's vitals kicked up a notch in response to being held.

"That's a strong heartbeat," Dante said. "She's a real fighter."

"Yes. She is." Shay ran her fingers over the tiny feet that had kicked her.

Her baby was alive.

"I thought I'd lost this," Shay whispered. "I hope I never feel that way again."

"Me too," Dante said. "It was the worst feeling ever. If I lost either of you… I couldn't go on living. You are both my heart. My loves."

"I feel the same," she whispered.

"*Cara*, our little girl needs a name. I wanted you to name her."

"Me?"

"*Sì.*"

"Sophia," Shay said without hesitation. "My mother's name and your long-lived *zia*. I hope you don't mind."

"I don't. That is a good first name and how about Maria for the second? That was my mother's name."

Shay nodded. "I like that."

"Sophia Maria Affini. Or rather Principessa Sophia. It has a nice ring to it."

"It does." Shay sighed. "I guess I should tender my resignation with the United World Wide Health Association."

"Why?" Dante asked.

"It seems I'll be staying in Italy for a while."

"You don't have to resign from the United World Wide Health Association."

"Why not?"

"Because I've tendered my resignation at the hospital. I have to give them six months' notice and finish up the work that you started."

"What?" she asked, surprised. "You resigned?"

"*Sì*, I joined the United World Wide Health Association as a trainer. I won't be doing any kind of missions that you used to do, because we have a child, but I will finish your work while you recover, and then in six months we'll head to America, where I will spend three months training trauma surgeons to head out to disaster zones. Then, who knows where we'll go? I was told that training can happen all over the world in various cities. The point is, we'll go together. The three of us. I requested that you will work alongside me. I can't work without you."

"But…but you love Italy."

"*Sì*, I do, but I love you more and your work is important to you. It's your passion and it's all you have, besides us. Anyways, Venice is our home base. We'll come back for summers on the Lido and Christmases in Tuscany. I have enough money to pick and choose when I want to work and where. Besides, time in Tuscany while you're healing will be nice. Serena and Guillermo can't wait to spoil this little girl. Italy is just a place we hang our hats. The three of us is what makes a home."

Shay smiled. Yes. Italy was a great place to live, as New Orleans had been. Just a place she'd passed through since her mother died, but her husband and her daughter were her life. Wherever they were together they were home. And for the first time in her life she had a home. Love and roots that were all her own.

* * * * *

Look out for the next great story in the
ROYAL SPRING BABIES *duet*

BABY SURPRISE FOR THE DOCTOR PRINCE
by Robin Gianna

And if you enjoyed this story,
check out these other great reads
from Amy Ruttan

ALEJANDRO'S SEXY SECRET
UNWRAPPED BY THE DUKE
TEMPTING NASHVILLE'S CELEBRITY DOC
PERFECT RIVALS...

All available now!

MILLS & BOON®
Large Print Medical

October

Their One Night Baby	Carol Marinelli
Forbidden to the Playboy Surgeon	Fiona Lowe
A Mother to Make a Family	Emily Forbes
The Nurse's Baby Secret	Janice Lynn
The Boss Who Stole Her Heart	Jennifer Taylor
Reunited by Their Pregnancy Surprise	Louisa Heaton

November

Mummy, Nurse...Duchess?	Kate Hardy
Falling for the Foster Mum	Karin Baine
The Doctor and the Princess	Scarlet Wilson
Miracle for the Neurosurgeon	Lynne Marshall
English Rose for the Sicilian Doc	Annie Claydon
Engaged to the Doctor Sheikh	Meredith Webber

December

Healing the Sheikh's Heart	Annie O'Neil
A Life-Saving Reunion	Alison Roberts
The Surgeon's Cinderella	Susan Carlisle
Saved by Doctor Dreamy	Dianne Drake
Pregnant with the Boss's Baby	Sue MacKay
Reunited with His Runaway Doc	Lucy Clark

MILLS & BOON®
Large Print Medical

January

The Surrogate's Unexpected Miracle	Alison Roberts
Convenient Marriage, Surprise Twins	Amy Ruttan
The Doctor's Secret Son	Janice Lynn
Reforming the Playboy	Karin Baine
Their Double Baby Gift	Louisa Heaton
Saving Baby Amy	Annie Claydon

February

Tempted by the Bridesmaid	Annie O'Neil
Claiming His Pregnant Princess	Annie O'Neil
A Miracle for the Baby Doctor	Meredith Webber
Stolen Kisses with Her Boss	Susan Carlisle
Encounter with a Commanding Officer	Charlotte Hawkes
Rebel Doc on Her Doorstep	Lucy Ryder

March

The Doctor's Forbidden Temptation	Tina Beckett
From Passion to Pregnancy	Tina Beckett
The Midwife's Longed-For Baby	Caroline Anderson
One Night That Changed Her Life	Emily Forbes
The Prince's Cinderella Bride	Amalie Berlin
Bride for the Single Dad	Jennifer Taylor